HOT WIND, BOILING RAIN

Scary Stories for Strong Hearts

Other Books By Lyn Ford

Beyond the Briar Patch
Affrilachian Folktales, Food and Folklore

Affrilachian Tales
Folktales from the African-American Appalachian Tradition

HOT WIND, BOILING RAIN

Scary Stories for Strong Hearts

LYN FORD

Honored by her peers as a
Circle of Excellence Storyteller
Of the National Storytelling Network

Parkhurst Brothers Publishers
MARION, MICHIGAN

www.parkhurstbrothers.com
Parkhurst Brothers books are distributed to the trade through the Chicago Distribution Center, and may be ordered through Ingram Book Company, Baker & Taylor, Follett Library Resources and other book industry wholesalers. To order from Chicago Distribution Center, phone 800-621-2736 or send a fax to 800-621-8476. Copies of this and other Parkhurst Brothers, Inc., Publishers titles are available to organizations and corporations for purchase in quantity by contacting Special Sales Department at our home office location, listed on our website. Manuscript submission guidelines for this publishing company are available at our website.

Printed in the United States of America
First Edition, 2015
2015 2016 2017 2018 2019 2020 16 15 14 13 12 11 10 9 8 7 6 5 4 3 2 1

Library of Congress Cataloging in Publication Data will appear in the space below after issuance.

ISBN: Trade Paperback 978162491-057-9
ISBN: e-book 978162491-058-6

Parkhurst Brothers Publishers believes that the free and open exchange of ideas is essential for the maintenance of our freedoms. We support the First Amendment of the United States Constitution and encourage all citizens to study all sides of public policy questions, making up their own minds. Closed minds cost a society dearly.

Cover and interior design by Linda D. Parkhurst, Ph.D.
Proofread by Bill and Barbara Paddack
Acquired for Parkhurst Brothers, Inc., Publishers by: Ted Parkhurst

032015

Dedicated to

Dad, for telling stories

Mom, for reading stories

Family, for being stories

Ancestors, whose lives became the roots of our stories

Our children, for creating and growing new stories

My beloved, for sharing my story

I challenged myself to write this.

Now I pass the challenge to you.

ACKNOWLEDGEMENTS

To those who have been the Wind, Water, Earth, and Fire of this endeavor:

Ted and Linda Parkhurst, who still believe in what I can do, even when I'm not sure I can do it. "Your deadline is ..."

Michael Reno Harrell, for coming up with the name "Sinful Ella" as we ate barbecue with Kim Weitkamp in Montgomery, Alabama, and for saying the line that helped me put "If the Shoe Fits" together: "This one ain't right. Gimme the one with the big feet!" I told the story first, Michael, and the young folks loved that line. Then I revamped the idea for the story in this book. I think it worked!

The folklorist Alan Dundes (Sept. 8, 1934-March 30, 2005), whose teachings and writings helped establish the study of folklore as an academic discipline.

Bruce, my "roadie" and best friend, who brought me pumpkin ice cream while I worked to complete this manuscript.

My family, and my extended family in storytelling, who always encourage me, including my friends in the Storytellers of Central Ohio, the Ohio Order for the Preservation of Storytelling, The Cleveland Association of Black Storytellers, The National Association of Black Storytellers, The National Storytelling Network, the Ohio Alliance for Arts Education, my "Sassy Sisters," and my big and little brothers everywhere.

THANK YOU.

Table of Contents

FOREWORD

"I'm going hunting for mysteries, cover me"

—Bjork, "Cover Me" (on Post CD, Elektra, 1995)

SINCE THE DAYS when I was an elementary school student, back in the time of the gigantic radio and the tiny television screen, I loved to watch old movies. Film noir, science fiction, and, especially, horror movies. I wasn't afraid of them, even when the shadows stretched from the screen into my imagination and dreams. Although the television images were in black and white, my dreams were very colorful.

I would awaken from one of those moving-in-slow-motion or can't seem-to-move-at-all dreams, and, even if it was a bit startling, I would immediately begin to analyze its content. An example: In the shadows of a bathroom with no light switch, did I see the Creature from the Black Lagoon stepping from behind the shower curtain, or was that the arm of Boris Karloff disguised as Frankenstein's monster? How did it get into the house, that monstrous and confusing thing, and why was it drooling peanut butter? Hmmm, interesting ...

Sometimes I would lie in my bed, listening to my little sister snoring in her bed beside mine, and my little brother snoring in his room, and my mother and my father snoring in their room. I wondered if I snored. Probably not, my ego told me; it also told me, as I continued to analyze that dream, "That was the noise you heard coming from the monster. Everybody is snoring! And the peanut butter? You're hungry. Go downstairs and sneak into the kitchen. Make yourself a peanut butter sandwich. Add grape jelly."

I did go downstairs. I did make a sandwich. I added grape jelly to the peanut butter. And I sat under the table in the darkness of our kitchen (which somehow felt safe), and created an ending for the story of the monster who devoured peanut butter sandwiches behind the shower curtain.

I decided he was Frankenstein's monster, with whom I felt a certain empathy. He was different from everyone else, as I was. I was a weird little bookworm who liked to draw and to sing for herself; I was the only child of color in our class of "gifted" students (but we weren't called "gifted" in those days. We were "the fast learners"). The monster was taunted and threatened, as I sometimes was. And on the night he crept into my mind, he was running from the people who chased him and wanted to destroy him. He got hungry. He made a peanut butter sandwich. And he hid in the bathtub, behind the shower curtain, in the dark bathroom of my dream.

And how did his story end? I decided that the monster had hidden in the bathroom, and, seeing me, knew we were kindred spirits. The monster took my hand. We walked out of the house and into the dark streets, then into the houses of those who teased me. My friend, the monster, made those snoring sounds to frighten my tormenters. I told them that the monster was my friend and did whatever I asked. Then he and I went back to my home, where I hid my friend under my bed. And the children in my class never teased me again.

A very satisfying conclusion. With my belly full of bread and peanut butter and jelly, and my mind content, I tiptoed back upstairs and crawled into bed. I slept deeply for at least an hour or two. Then the sun rose, and my mother's alarm clock shattered the silence and my dreams, and the day began.

I was never afraid of the night, for I had my monster under my bed. And my great-grandmother, Essie Arkward, had told me not to be afraid of ghosts.

"Dead folks don't bother you much," she said. "It's the livin' folks you need to worry about."

"There are things that are known and things that are unknown; in between are doors."

I became acquainted with Edgar Alan Poe and William Shakespeare and Washington Irving as I read old books in my safe haven on the branch of our cherry tree when I was in third grade. I was enchanted by Saki (H.H. Munro) and Ray Bradbury every summer after I discovered their work on the adult shelves of the library. To reach those shelves, when I was considered too young to check out adult books, I crawled on my belly like a commando from the children's section, beyond the desk of the children's librarian. I stealthily passed, still on my belly, the high desk of the head librarian, and made my way to sit and read on the floor in the stacks of grown-up literature, or to sneak an "adult" book back to the children's section, and hide it on a shelf there when I'd finished with it.

Looking back on the whole stealth-for-stories scenarios, I now believe that the head librarian knew what I was doing all along. She never said anything about it, but there was something in the way she smiled at me, and the suggestions she made for my reading material when I received my teen library card.

When I was a teenager, I began to write haunting stories. I hid them from my family and the few friends I had. Sometimes I tore them up and threw them away. I figured folks already thought I was a bit strange. Why give them proof? The stories probably weren't particularly good, but now I wish I'd kept them.

My original tales of terror usually ended with someone's well-deserved death, often at the hands of a vengeful ghost. These tales of the macabre were influenced by the work of authors (and later, actors) who became as familiar to me as the monster under my bed. They served the purpose of both venting my frustrations and creatively expressing myself.

My father, Edward Maclin Cooper, gave me a good foundation in creepy stories, which he sometimes told at bedtime to the horror of my sister and brother and to my great satisfaction.

My grandfather, Byard Wilmer Arkward, added to that foundation a few tales he claimed were true. One was about a wicked and hypocritical group of church-goers, who died when a flash of lightning burned their church to the ground. Another was about a game of cards with Mr. Scratch (Lucifer). A third one was my grandfather's tale of getting drunk and finding a talking head on the railroad tracks, which made him instantly sober, according to him. When I said a ghost tale or a tall tale or one of his blatant lies just couldn't be true, Pop-pops would say, "Well if it ain't true, it should be."

I developed a taste for The Alfred Hitchcock Hour, Rod Serling's Twilight Zone, and Thriller, a program hosted by my buddy, Boris Karloff. I also relished Karloff's shriveled personification of the Mummy, and Bela Lugosi's Dracula, shown on late-night TV, if I could get the rabbit-ears antenna to pick up a channel signal transmitted from Cleveland, Ohio.

As I grew up, I fell in love with Vincent Price and Christopher Lee and Cousin Itt (the Addams family's fuzzy little relative, who wore a distinctive bowler hat), and I tried to walk with my arms folded and my feet mincing along in that strangely sophisticated and sexy manner that was Morticia Addams' signature step. The Addams Family and The Munsters were family favorites. Even my mom and my little sister, who was terrified by eyeballs and darkness and creepy voices, watched those two television shows.

All this was background material for my own telling of what Dad called "spookers and haints" tales. But my greatest source for horror stories was the collection of folktales by the

Brothers Grimm. Nothing matched the fair maidens in tragic circumstances, the innocent children in horrid situations, the cruel villains and gruesome deaths and the divine justice I found on the pages of the thick book of stories that sat in the adult section of the library on the shelves marked 398.2. I had read everything on the shelves in the children's section, and thanks to my commando raids, many of the works on the shelves of the adult section. Children weren't supposed to be in the adult section, but I'd been there since third grade. So, when I received my own, official "adult" library card at the age of thirteen, I grabbed that book of unedited, too-untidy-for-tots Grimm tales and brought it home. If my mother had known what I was reading, she might have taken it back to the library. These were not stories sugared with Disney sweetness. These were the old tales translated from their German sources into a very mature form of American Business English.

These stories, as well as the works of many authors and story collectors —William J. Faulkner, Zora Neale Hurston, Washington Irving, Charles Perrault, Edgar Allan Poe, Ray Bradbury, to name a few —as well as the skills of my family of storytellers, were and are resources for the writing you find in this book. I don't hide the stories anymore.

I remember the excitement of discovering the dark reworking of folktales authored by Angela Carter, and the excitement of creating my own, as I did when the monster stepped from behind the shower curtain. I become acquainted with my monsters, and I play with them, making them my friends, making their stories a part of my own. I revise by first speaking the stories again and again for anyone who will listen, often on moonlit October nights. Then I adapt them from orature to literature, for in the telling of their stories, my characters become flesh and bone, mist and magic. They find their own voices; they walk their own paths. I walk with them until I know them well enough to revisit them on paper. For me, establishing such a relationship takes a lot of work.

I hope you can hear the voice of the storyteller in the literary format on these pages. I've given a lot of thought to the way I "speak story" and how and why I might write these narratives. I've also given you the source tales for my personal variants, and perhaps these source tales can become a foundation for your own story reconstruction. You may discover your own monsters along the way.

Make them your friends.

I love my monsters, my ghosts, my strange little children. I hope you love them, too.

"Don't turn on the light. It's not real when it's light.
It's only real when it's dark ... dark, and still."

– Charlotte Hollis, played by Bette Davis in *Hush, Hush, Sweet Charlotte* (Studio: The Associates and Aldrich; Distributed by 20th Century Fox, 1965)

OCTOBER NIGHT

October night
moon wild and bright
round as the owl's eyes
autumn sighs
listen
dying leaves hint at
mysteries whispered
from the roots hidden
in cool dark earth
things buried
still dream stories
that began
when nothing ever lived ...
Once upon a time ...
Once ... upon a ... time ...

THE BEGINNING: MY FIRST TWISTED TALE

I WAS TEN years old. On a particular evening, when I was supposed to be working on my math homework, my sister begged me to tell her a story. "Please, please, oh, please, oh please, oh, please, oh, please, oh please!"

Obviously, it was impossible to concentrate on the homework. And mathematics was beyond puzzling for me. It was confusing, and frustrating, and I was never much good at it. So, with frustration hissing from between my teeth and malice in my ten-year-old heart, I asked my sister, "What story do you want me to tell?"

My sister, five years younger than I, red-headed like our daddy, and always cute, even when she was annoying, smiled and sweetly said, "Tell me the story of the three bears."

I began my adaptation of ...

THE THREE BEARS

Once upon a time, there were three bears, a mama bear, a papa bear, and a wee little baby bear. They lived in a little bitty cottage in the forest.

My sister said, “That’s right.”

One morning, Mama Bear made porridge, you know, oatmeal stuff, but it was too hot to eat. So the three bears left their bowls of porridge on the table, and went for a walk in the forest. And they forgot to lock their front door, left it wide open.

My sister said, “That’s right.”

And while they were gone, along came a little girl with big golden curls. She saw that the bears had left their front door open, and being a snoopy little girl, she walked right into their house.

My sister said, “That’s right.”

She sat down in their chairs and broke Baby Bear’s chair. Then she went in the kitchen and tasted their porridge, and she ate Baby Bear’s porridge and licked the bowl clean. Then she went upstairs and tried out all their beds. One bed was too hard. One bed was too soft. One bed was just right; it was Baby Bear’s crib, with a soft blanket and a teddy bear in it. That little girl climbed into Baby Bear’s crib, and she curled up underneath that blanket and hugged that teddy bear and went to sleep ... zzzzz.

My sister seemed to be analyzing that part of my storytelling, but after some thought, she said, “That’s right.”

And while that little girl was sleeping, the three bears came home. They saw their front door, wide open. They thought somebody might be in the house, so they tiptoed up the stairs and into the living room. They looked all around.

Then Papa Bear said, “Somebody’s been sittin’ in my chair.”

Mama Bear said, "Somebody's been sitting in my chair."

Baby Bear said, "Aw, somebody's been sitting in my chair, and they broke it into toothpicks! Waaaah!"

My sister said, "Uh ... that's right."

The three bears tiptoed into the kitchen, to see if somebody was there. They looked all around.

Then Papa Bear said, "Somebody's been eatin' my porridge."

Mama Bear said, "Somebody's been eating my porridge."

Baby Bear said, "Aw, somebody's been eating my porridge, and they ate it all gone! Waaaah!"

My sister said, "Um ... that's right."

Now, the three bears knew somebody had been in the house. They tiptoed upstairs. They looked all around.

Papa Bear said, "Somebody's been sleepin' in my bed."

Mama Bear said, "Somebody's been sleeping in my bed."

Baby Bear said, "Aw, somebody's been sleeping in my bed, and she's still there! Look! It's a little girl, with golden curls!"

And then ... and I turned directly toward my sister, and looked deeply and menacingly into her eyes ... and then ... I leaned forward, so that I could whisper ...

And then ... the three bears ATE GOLDILOCKS!

My little sister grabbed her long, red braids. Her eyes grew wide and round like a frog's. She breathed in quickly and said, "UH UH!"

I replied, "Yes, they did."

"UH UH! Mommy read me that story, and she didn't say the three bears ate Goldilocks!"

"Well, maybe Mommy didn't want to scare you. Maybe she didn't know what happened. But I do. The three bears ate Goldilocks."

"UH UH!"

"Yes, they did. And ever since the three bears ate Goldilocks, they've been lurking in the darkness of the night, and roaming the streets, looking for more tender, juicy little girls too eat."

"UH UH!"

"Yep." I was enjoying this entirely too much. I went on. "The three bears especially like the ones with golden curls, or long ... red ... braids."

My poor little sister looked at the ends of her braids, held tightly in her little fists ..." UH UH!"

"Yep," I said again. "But, you know, the three bears never bother little girls, if they're already asleep in their own beds."

My sister slowly let go of her braids. After a few seconds of silence, she said, "I think I'll go get ready for bed now." And, ZOOM! She was up the stairs.

I returned to my math homework, with a great sense of pride growing in my cruel and egotistical ten-year-old brain. I knew I had learned the power of voice and facial expression, and how to use the tools of tone and pacing and inflection. I recognized a connection to the skills of my favorite spooky storyteller, our dad. I felt quite satisfied with the outcome of what I'd done.

Then my sister told my mother.

That's another story.

—A NOTE OR TWO FOR YOU—

Synopsis of the old tale:

Since their breakfast cereal is too hot to eat, a family of three bears decides to go for a walk in the forest. They leave their front door open, and a snoopy little golden-haired girl walks in and: vandalizes the property by breaking furniture; commits robbery by eating the prepared breakfast, and becomes a squatter, crawling into someone else's bed and going to sleep. The Bear family returns to find their door open, their privacy invaded, and their house occupied by a stranger. The girl awakens to see the bears staring at her. She jumps out a window and escapes, and the story ends.

Yawn.

In my mind, that girl was an invader, the "other" who showed no respect for someone else's property and home. And what kind of common sense did she show by skipping alone through the forest and deliberately wandering into a stranger's cottage? She deserved being devoured. And in my adaptation, told to my sister, the cute little girl who was invading my space and denying me my homework-time, she was.

My sister says she doesn't remember this story. And yet, she speaks of me scaring her, and her eyes grow a bit wider ...

Old variant's motif:

AT 171, wild animals and humans

IF THE SHOE FITS—OR—SINFUL ELLA

BOB PRINCE WAS the first member of the Prince family to go to college. His daddy had made money the old-fashioned way, through other people's hard work. Bob's daddy had bought land and gotten other folks to farm it, financed mines and mills and hired other folks to labor, married into a wealthy family, bought into deals with men of substance and power, and become a kind of king in his own county. Daddy Prince had never seen a need to go to college. But he'd made sure his only child went, and rubbed elbows with the sons of other powerful men.

Then Daddy Prince died, leaving behind a grieving widow, a sad son, a large fortune, and a stipulation that Bob (legal name: Robert Aloysius Prince, Jr.) must finish school with honors, and marry into one of the other big-name families by his twenty-third birthday, or the money that didn't belong to the Widow Prince would go to a favored nephew, the well-mannered, popular and dashing Louis Weems, who already enjoyed an allowance bigger than some folks' yearly income. In that case, Bob would inherit a small piece of land to work and the money to start working it, a horse of his choosing, and the old shotgun Daddy Prince kept filled with rock salt and concealed in a trunk in the barn.

Louis had been treated like a son by Bob's namesake. Bob, always a picky, somewhat lazy child and overprotected by his mother, had been treated more like the offspring of a distant relative than an heir to his father's wealthy estate. And Bob had enjoyed the company of his mother's friends at their afternoon teas and soirées much more than he had his father's.

Mind you, I said he enjoyed their company, not their work.

When Daddy Prince's will was read, Bob was done with college. He'd graduated with honors (whether or not he deserved them was a questionable matter, since he was too lazy to study much, and his grades had been atrocious), and a reputation as a bit of a prude. His head was supposedly filled with knowledge, but knowledge doesn't necessarily make one skilled in living a life. Unlike his cousin Louis, who spoke quite eloquently of love and lust and everything else, and had attended the same Ivy League school but spent most of his evenings in rendezvous at the ladies' finishing school down the road from it, Bob had never so much as smiled at a woman. Bob was twenty-two years old, mere days away from turning twenty-three, with no prospects for marriage whatsoever.

So he turned to his mother for advice. "Mother," he asked, with his head on her knee, "How can I find a wife before my twenty-third birthday? It's just days away!" Bob whined as he spoke, knowing this would bring the best response from his mother.

"Well, my darling boy," his mother doted, "my only suggestion would be to visit all the neighboring families and see which ones have daughters you might marry. If you move quickly, if you ride through the county tomorrow and use your greeting and your first conversation as your courtship, you may have a proposal to make by midnight. But there aren't many prospects for marriage around here. Louis may know of some families with suitable young ladies. Ask Louis to ride with you, dear."

Riding all over the county sounded like work to Bob. He pouted a bit. Pouting might help his mother come up with an easier plan.

"But, Mother, how will I know if a girl is the right one for me? I want someone who will treat me the way you do. And she has to be a proper lady." Bob gently stroked his mother's tiny foot. She sighed. Then she patted Bob on the head.

"Oh, I have a wonderful idea!" Widow Prince giggled like a little girl. "When you patted my foot, it came to me! There was a handsome young man who used to sit at my feet, and pat them. He was my very first suitor. He said I had the daintiest ankles ... well, never mind that.

"I have a pair of golden slippers that I wore on my wedding day, and a golden bag to match them. The bag doesn't matter right now, but the shoes! If a young woman's feet are as small and delicate as mine, then she will undoubtedly be a fine choice for a wife for you, for she won't have worked in the fields or around the house. She will have sat at the piano, or tatted lace collars and doilies, and carried on polite conversations with other fine young ladies. She will have been raised as a lady should be!"

Widow Prince shoved her son away from her feet, and practically skipped to the cedar chest at the foot of her bed. It had been her hope trunk, a part of her dowry, and it held all the mementos of her wedding day —the gown, the petticoats, a blue garter, the pearl necklace she had borrowed from her Aunt Viola and never returned, the ivory fan she had carried with her bridal bouquet, the golden slippers, as bright and shiny as they were when her own mother bought them, and the matching gold purse with the pearl-encrusted clasp.

Widow Prince gave the slippers and the purse to Bob. "Find Louis, tell him the plan for my shoes," she said, "and make your arrangements for tomorrow. Louis will be your best man, of course, so it is fitting that he should ride with you. And the proper bride will not refuse these gifts from her future mother-in-law. Oh, this will go well. You will be married on your birthday!"

Bob trotted to Louis' apartment in the west wing of the house. His mother's plan sounded as if it might work, and riding along with Louis would surely make the journey a hasty one. Louis probably knew all the young women of marriageable age in the county. Why, he probably knew which one would fit into those little golden shoes.

Louis did. The next morning, Bob and Louis, dressed in their finest clothes and riding the best white stallions from Daddy Prince's stables, went to only one farm, the Wallop's.

Caesar Wallop and his second wife, Irma, had the second largest farm in the county, and the prettiest daughter in the state, too. There were two daughters, in fact —Irma's firstborn, Gladys, and Ella, Irma's beautiful child with Caesar.

The two girls were as different as day and night. Both were a feast for the eyes of any young man. But Gladys was tall and big-boned, broad of shoulder and hip and toe, doe-eyed and quiet and contented to work in the kitchen with the servants and laugh with the field hands for whom they cooked. Gladys also liked to read dime novels about the Wild West, or Robert Service's Songs of the Sourdough or Spell of the Yukon and Other Verses, which she concealed in her Bible while reading them. That was her only vice.

Gladys had been courted by a hardworking young man by the name of Luther "Stubby" Davenport. He read the same books that Gladys loved, and decided that the Yukon Territory was meant to be his home. Stubby proposed to Gladys, and when she hesitated to reply, he told her that she must marry him immediately, or be left behind, for he would be gone soon to the Yukon Territory.

"It's now or never, Gladys," he said. And Gladys replied, "Well, Stubby, then I guess it's never. I will marry by choice and proposal, not by a threat."

Stubby was stunned, but he left, and found himself writing to Gladys every day.

Ella received letters every day, too. They were proposals of a different kind —small notes with big promises and directions for trysting places. Ella never refused a tryst. She was small and well-formed from her perfect golden curls to her dainty hands and feet. She rarely worked at anything except the latest song or dance, or a glass of good liquor. She didn't walk into bars, she sauntered and sashayed into private rooms behind curtains or at the back of inns. There, she would bat her thick eyelashes in a way that made a man's heart flutter and his common sense fly, along with his money. He would propose, and Ella would say, "Let's get married now!"

Ella eloped about once every three or four months, but the elopements "didn't take," as her father put it. In a few days, Ella would be returned to the Wallop's farm. She was a bit mussed and not quite sober, yet she seemed none the worse for wear. She always returned smiling, laden with gifts and a supply of cash, and unmarried.

Of course, Louis knew of Ella's reputation. He had not eloped with Ella, but he'd come close to it. This he did not tell Bob.

What he told Bob was that he knew of an exceedingly beautiful young woman who was as dainty as a rose and who would love to be wed. When Bob saw Ella sitting on the porch with her family, he nearly fell off his horse. He recovered from his clumsiness by stepping forward and falling to one knee and pronouncing, "I've come in search of a bride."

Irma jumped up from her rocking chair and shoved Gladys down the porch steps. "Here's one! She's a good 'un. She'll make you a fine bride. She's been mopin' around here for months and months, and I'd love to see her married!"

Bob looked at Gladys. Pretty smile, grand figure, but her feet were almost as big as his.

"No, I can't ask for this one's hand. Her feet are too

big. That's a bad sign," Bob said. Then he realized everyone was confusedly staring at him, and he still had his mother's shoes in his pockets. He drew them out and showed them to Irma and Gladys, and to Ella, who sashayed up, grinned, and blinked those eyelashes a few times.

"My mother offers these shoes to my bride-to-be. If they fit, then she's a lady, and that's the woman for me," Bob explained.

Louis remained on his horse, embarrassed by his cousin's unmannerly proposal. Caesar Wallop stepped off the porch and said, "Boy, that don't make sense. But you might try those shoes on Ella here."

Ella had already removed her own shoes and was trying on one of the golden slippers. She did her best not to salivate at their silken shine and the idea of their cost. She was mentally working out a list of folks to invite to her wedding —"ladies" she'd met at some of the taverns and men who enjoyed their company and hers, but not her family of country bumpkins. There'd be no elopement this time, Ella thought, for elopements did not offer opportunities for the kind of party this proposing idiot and his mother might be able to afford.

Irma gasped, and Gladys shook her head, as Ella happily said, "Oh, the shoe fits!"

Ella didn't even know Bob's name when she kissed him full on the mouth. Bob was so taken aback, he barely heard her father say, "She's been proposed to a lot, this one. But the potential grooms always bring her back. She's a handful, I'll grant you that. Sometimes I think she just ain't right. Seems like her weddings just don't take. Hope this one does."

Irma nodded so quickly, her head seemed to vibrate. She waved goodbye to her troublesome daughter and future son-in-law, and whoever that other young man was. Then she started running for the garden shed, where she'd kept items she had hoped would make a fine dowry for one of her daughters. Gladys stood in the front yard alone. On the ground in front of her lay a small, golden purse.

Ella rode nestled in front of Bob on the softest saddle and the finest horse she'd ever seen. Every now and then, she glanced at the fellow on the other horse. He looked familiar.

When they got back to the Prince estate, Ella was swept up to Mrs. Prince's bedroom. Out of the cedar trunk came the old wedding gown, still pristine and white. It fit Ella as if it had been made for her. Widow Prince squealed with glee, and plans for a wedding and reception went forth from that very moment.

Bob embraced Louis, thanking him for his help. "This guarantees that the family fortune goes to me, not you, Louis! I will be married on my birthday! That's only a few days from now! I'm going to be married to a fine lady! I'm going to be the lord of the land!" Bob blurted.

Louis stopped smiling, but only for a moment. He knew that he would still live in the Prince home, the fanciest "farmhouse" in the state. He would still receive the allowance Daddy Prince had endowed for his lifetime. And Ella, with whom he was definitely acquainted, would now live there, too.

Louis grinned, and heartily slapped Bob on the back.

On the wedding day, things got as confused as that

proposal Bob had made. The servants couldn't get their work done for all the commands and curses Ella threw at them. Bob paced back and forth in his chambers. Every now and then he muttered, "Maybe this isn't a good idea. Maybe I should just be willing to —oh, I can't say it —work." Louis strutted about, humming Felix Mendelssohn's "Wedding March" and winking at the maids and the cooks and the doormen.

Widow Prince started sipping brandy as soon as she woke up. She told her maid that she didn't think Ella was a fit bride for her son.

"That girl wants to have the reception before the wedding!" Widow Prince whined. "Before the wedding! And I do believe she has already had the wedding night, but I'm not sure it was with my son!" Widow Prince chugged more brandy, and held out the snifter to her maid, who tried her best not to snicker.

Ella really didn't want to wait until after the wedding to have a reception. She'd invited her friends to come over early and help her toast the occasion and open gifts a day before the servants had started decorating the house. Ella had also ordered up a New Orleans jazz band (at Bob's expense). She'd heard them playing at some nearby festivity, and insisted they stay in the Prince's guest house, and come up to the farmhouse to play some tunes while she and her friends drank the high-quality bourbon and the imported champagne that was meant for the post-ceremony celebration.

When she was finally dressed, Bob's mother brought her wedding present downstairs to Ella. Ella snatched it from her, opened it, and laughed. "Mother Prince," Ella snickered, "We won't be needing that!" And all Ella's guests laughed, too. "That" was an antique, ornately crafted bed warmer.

The only "friend" of Ella that Bob knew was Louis, who seemed to be well-acquainted with the bride-to-be. Louis and Ella kissed a bit too long and hard, and touched one another in intimate ways. Bob tried not to stare, but he could feel his face growing warm and his hands getting sweaty every time he saw his cousin and his betrothed together.

The wedding presents ranged from the beautiful to the bizarre. From the Wallop family came a rare Bakhtiari rug from Persia. Ella immediately had it unrolled beneath the French bronze and crystal chandelier that her father and mother had delivered and hung earlier in the week, to light the wedding space. That was before they knew they weren't invited to the wedding.

Louis had two gifts delivered, too. One was an ornate mirror in a gold frame highlighted by naked cherubs and cabbage roses. The other was a plaster statuette, rather cheap compared to the rest of the gifts. Bob examined it closely as Ella set it on the foyer table. The face looked very much like Ella's, but Bob wasn't sure about the figure. It was naked.

That statue disturbed Bob. He needed to do something to take his mind off what he was thinking. He decided he'd go get the minister.

"Ella, darling," he said, "I'm going to pick up Reverend White. I'll be back in plenty of time to get dressed for the wedding."

Bob hitched the white stallions to the wagon, which was decorated with ribbons and floral bouquets. As he climbed into the wagon and turned the horses toward the road, he heard the band tuning up and Ella's friends laughing raucously.

When Bob came back, he just sat in the wagon. Reverend White looked at the house, then at Bob, then back toward the house, which was spewing noise like a raging flood, with loud bursts of screams and curses and laughter, and thunderous music.

The minister got down from the wagon first. "Son," he said to Bob, "let me go in and settle things down a bit. It sounds like that pre-wedding celebrating you told me about is getting out of hand. The presence of a holy man may remind those in attendance that a wedding is a sacred occasion."

Reverend White walked solemnly to and into the house. The noise stopped, but only for a few minutes. Reverend White came running back toward the wagon. He passed it; and slowing his pace a bit and trying to catch his breath, he sternly walk up to the road. He shouted, "Bob, look to your woman before she walks down the aisle, and discern her nature! And know that I will not perform any wedding ceremony today!"

Reverend White kept shouting something about "travesty" and "abomination" as he loped down the road.

Bob cautiously walked into his home and understood what the minister had meant. For there was Ella in her gold slippers and her white wedding gown. But it was difficult to tell how she'd look walking down the aisle. She was swinging upside-down from the chandelier over the Bakhtiari rug. She was whooping and hollering with her bloomers showing as her petticoats and dress covered the rest of her like a lampshade, while singing songs that should not be sung in polite company. The room was filled with laughing "well-wishers," drunkenly reeling as much as they were dancing, while the jazz band played a version of "Frankie and Johnny," offbeat and in three different bourbon-soaked key signatures.

Bob found the servants hiding in the kitchen. They were ashamed of the ruined wedding, they said, and afraid of the wedding party. But they were not sure what to do about any of it.

Bob stormed out the back door. Where was his mother? Bob found her plopped down on Daddy Prince's grave.

Mama Prince was sitting inside the little white picket fence that guarded the grave. She'd lost her shoes and stockings and sat with her bare toes curled and her antique bed warmer in her gloved hands. She kept bashing the ground with that heavy thing, thud, thud, thud, and wailing, "Chester, I knew it all along! (Thud.) You were a gentleman, not a money-grubbing social climber! (Thud.) You loved my ankles! (Thud.) Chester, I should have married you!" (Thud, thud, thud.)

Bob wondered who Chester was. No matter. There were other things to deal with now. He passed Widow Prince, left her sitting on her dead husband. He went to the barn and came back to the house with his daddy's old shotgun, loaded with rock salt.

The shotgun was used three times. First time, Bob shattered the cheap plaster statue of the naked woman. The second shot spattered the gaudy mirror with the little naked angels flying around the frame.

Then Bob aimed at Ella, still swinging from the chandelier. She looked at him cross-eyed, and shouted, "That's right, Bobby!

Make some noise! Whoopee!!!"

Bob came to his senses. He took a deep breath, said a small prayer, and swung that shotgun toward Louis Weems' rapidly departing backside. "This is your doing, Louis," Bob calmly said. "Dainty feet mean she's a lady, huh? You know a girl with dainty feet, huh?"

When that rock salt stung his trousers, Louis whinnied like a filly and bolted out the door. And all the "well-wishers" followed him as quickly as they could.

Bob dropped the gun and looked toward the chandelier again. With a shout of "Wheeee," Ella somersaulted from it to the floor. She landed as if she was an experienced acrobat. Then she belched, and threw up on the Bakhtiari rug.

"Whew," she sighed. "Now, that was a party! Husband mine, what should we do next?"

Bob knew what he should do next. And he did it. He figured he'd have to hurry, if he wanted to be married before his birthday was over.

Evening sunlight stretched across the fields when Bob and Ella showed up at the Wallop farmhouse. Bob helped Ella down from the wagon. She limped and groaned a bit. Seems that landing wasn't quite as acrobatic as Bob had thought. Ella was sobering up, and her tiny ankles were swollen and hurt almost as much as her head. She'd stained and torn Widow Prince's wedding dress, and she'd lost one of those golden slippers.

Big Daddy Wallop came out on the porch. It only took two seconds for him to figure out that Ella was back to stay. "Guess that weddin' thing didn't take, did it?" he asked Bob.

Bob shook his head. "This one, as you put it, 'just ain't right,' Mr. Wallop," he said. "Quick, gimme the one with the big feet!"

But Bob's prospects of inherited fortune were gone, as was the one with the big feet. She'd made up her mind to go someplace where family fortunes and feet didn't matter quite as much. She'd gotten another letter from Stubby, and he was still interested in marrying her.

"But this time, I give you free reign to decide if that's what you want," his latest letter said. "I know you're a good and smart woman, Gladys. And I know I miss you more than I can say, and I love you, and I'll wait as long as it takes for you to forgive me and my big mouth. If you can, and you're willing to come up to Alaska and marry me, I promise you a fine house of your own and all that might make you feel comfortable. We'll cook together, we'll work together, we'll read together. You won't need a dowry, but you know you never did for me. I never cared one whit about your family's money. But I am rich now myself, for I struck the mother lode here, and I'll want for nothing, except you.

"If you don't write back, I'll know I've lost the best woman in the world. But if you do, I'll be ready to come and fetch you quicker than a hummingbird can fly."

Gladys had written a letter to Stubby, but she was on her way to the Yukon Territory and she was carrying that letter to him. It was in her carpetbag, in a little gold purse that used to match a pair of golden slippers too small for Gladys to wear.

—A NOTE OR TWO FOR YOU—

This is a pretty big spin-off from the usual "Cinderella" fare. Yet it meets the older criteria of some folklorists for stories classified as "Cinderellaesque." Rather than give one synoptic version of the old tale, I'll share some details that might be of more importance for a potential tale-twisting storyteller:

In 1893, Marian Rolafe Cox compared cultural similarities and relevant concepts for stories that could be classified as Cinderella tales. These wonder tales usually ended in "happily ever after," and approached that ending through an adventure that begins with a protagonist facing family problems and some magical intervention. Cox was commissioned by the Folklore Society of Britain to study every Cinderellaesque variant known at the time. The result was her work, *Cinderella: Three Hundred and Forty-Five Variants of Cinderella, Catskin and Cap o'Rushes, Abstracted and Tabulated with a Discussion of Medieval Analogues and Notes* (London: David Nutt for The Folklore Society, Strand, 1893).

Cox had no definitive folklore index or collected works to help her. With some critical and creative thinking, she managed to deduce five broad categories for the variants she discovered:

A—Cinderella (the protagonist as ill-treated heroine, who is recognized by means of a shoe). The persecuted girl receives some kind of magical assistance or help from some uncommon source or sources. By the end of the tale, she has reached a social status through marriage.

B—Catskin (the protagonist suffers due to an unnatural father, resulting in her flight). The father is neglectful and incestuous (or proposing incest). His actions cause the protagonist to flee and disguise herself in some skin (donkey, cat, fur, etc.). The girl runs away, finds a lover, and is safe. This variant became one of the most censored versions of the tale.

C—Cap o'Rushes (the protagonist experiences a "King Lear" judgment and is cast out). The father misjudges his daughter's character and abandons her or casts her out. This "Cinderella" is akin to Cordelia in William Shakespeare's "King Lear"; her sisters are likened to the two wicked stepsisters.

D—Indeterminate. This is the bag into which we can throw all those stories that hold some mixture of the story's typical elements: the protagonist's abuse, neglect, ostracism; magical animals and elements; benevolent mentors; marriage into a higher social status or marriage to someone who recognizes something about the protagonist that makes her a worthy spouse, etc.

E—Hero Tales (the protagonist is a male character who suffers a plight and plot similar to Cinderella). The protagonist is male. The story adheres in some way to the Cinderella motif.

Folklore indexes and fairytale anthologies were developed in the late 1800s and throughout the 1900s (and they are still studied, tweaked, expanded, and debated). In 1932, R. D. Jameson, who was a professor at the National Tsing Hua University at the time, became aware of the Chinese variant "Yeh-hsein." In his work, Jameson cited what he considered five clearly succinct elements of a Cinderella variant:

1. A young girl is ill treated.
2. She is forced to do menial service at home or abroad.
3. She meets a prince or a prince becomes aware of her beauty.
4. She is identified by her shoe.
5. She marries the prince.[1]

In 1951, Swedish folklorist Anna Brigitta Rooth published her doctoral dissertation known as "The Cinderella Cycle." This dissertation examined seven hundred variants of the Cinderella story and included distinctive subtypes. Rooth attempted to determine and clarify the story's original type, and how the story was disseminated. The works of Rooth and Cox are still valued references among folklorists who remain interested in a tale that has traveled, transformed, and survived as a shared transcultural tale.[2]

For the serious student of Cinderellaesque tales, more information than you can shake a shoe at is available on the Internet. Also, look for Alan Dundes' *Cinderella, a Folklore Casebook* (New York: Garland Publishing, Inc., 1982, or University of Wisconsin Press, 1988).

Old variant's motif:

ATU510, Persecuted Heroine (or Cinderella)

1. FOLKLORISTS CRITERIA FOR #510. http://www.artic.edu/webspaces/510iftheshoefits/2criteria.html
2. Ibid.

RED

ON THE NIGHT of my thirteenth birthday, I sat at my grandmother's feet and admired the opal ring she had given me. Sparks rose from the low fire in the fireplace. The full moon cast a soft light through the window.

"Grandmother," I said, "please tell me a story for my birthday. Please tell me my favorite story."

Grandmother sat back in her chair, closed her eyes, and began, "It was the evening of my own thirteenth birthday. Yes, I was just your age. I was walking through the forest to my own grandmother's house. She was going to give me a family heirloom for my birthday, an old opal ring. I was taking a basket of good things to her —soup, honey, a bottle of wine, and bread that was still warm. In the basket I also carried my father's hunting knife. Father had told me there was a wolf in the forest.

"I was wearing the gift she had made for me, a fine red-hooded coat.

"'Wear this when you come to visit me,' she had said. 'It

will keep you warm and safe in the woods.'

"The sky was graying, turning black. A soft rain fell, just enough to make the forest whisper. Then I heard another sound, a rustling in the bushes next to the path. Something watched me as I walked. I stopped, and reached into the basket for my father's knife.

"A wolf burst from the bushes. It leapt toward me. I swung my father's knife. The creature howled and ran off, leaving its paw, bleeding and quivering on the path.

"I heard the wolf's cry. I could tell it was running toward my grandmother's house. So I ran, too, as quickly as I could. When I got to the house, the door was open; it had no lock. I rushed inside.

"My grandmother was in bed. She trembled as if fevered. The bed covers, soaking wet, were drawn up over her shaking body and head.

"'Grandmother,' I said, 'there's a wolf in the forest! But don't worry. I'm going to get Father. I'll be back as quickly as I can. I'll leave my basket just inside the door. I'll pull it close; maybe it can keep the door closed. Don't worry, Grandmother. Everything will be all right.'

"I set the basket inside the door as I stepped back outside into the rain. I pulled the basket toward me, to keep the door shut as far as possible. Then I ran, still holding my father's knife. I ran back up the path toward my home.

"I tried not to look at the thing I'd left on the path. I didn't want to see at it again. I tried not to see the blood, the paw ...

"It was gone. In its place there lay the hand of an old woman. And on its finger was my grandmother's opal ring.

"We buried Grandmother that night. And whenever anyone asked what had happened, Father said a wolf had eaten her."

The story ended. Grandma opened her eyes, and smiled at me. For a while, we watched the fire burning lower, and the moon rising higher in a perfect sky.

"Grandmother," I said, "I love that story. Is it true?"

"As true as any story can be," Grandmother said. "As true as the fire is warm. As true as the full moon's light shining through the window ...

"As true as the opal ring on your finger."

I said, "The moonlight is beautiful. It's as if the moon shines just for me tonight. Just for me, on my thirteenth birthday. But, Grandmother ... I feel ... so ... strange ... "

—A NOTE OR TWO FOR YOU—

Synopsis of one of the old variants:

Little Red Riding Hood

From the version collected and rewritten by Charles Perrault

Once upon a time there lived in a little village a very pretty little girl, the prettiest creature who was ever seen. Her grandmother had a little red riding hood made for her. It suited the girl well, and soon everybody called her Little Red Riding Hood.

One day Little Red Riding Hood's mother said to her, "Go and see how your grandmother is doing, for I hear she has been ill. Take her some cake, and a pot of butter." Little Red Riding Hood set off immediately to see her grandmother, who lived far away.

On her way through the wood, she met a wolf, who asked her where she was going. In her innocence, she said to him, "I am going to see my grandmother."

"Well, I'd like to see her, too," said the wolf, "You go this way, and I'll go that way, and we'll shall see who gets there first."

The wolf took the shortest path and ran as fast as he could; he arrived at Grandmother's house, and knocked at the door. In a childish voice, he claimed he was Little Red Riding Hood. And Grandmother, who was in bed, invited him to enter.

The wolf let himself into the house, and gobbled up Grandmother. Then he shut the door and got into the old woman's bed.

Soon after, along came Little Red Riding Hood. She knocked at the door.

"Who's there?" asked the wolf.

Little Red Riding Hood decided, after hearing that voice, that her grandmother had a cold. She answered, "It's Little Red Riding Hood. I've brought you some cake and butter."

The wolf called to her, "Open the door, and come in."

Little Red Riding Hood came in, and was bidden by the wolf, "Set the cake and the pot of butter on the stool, and come get into bed with me."

Little Red Riding Hood took off her clothes and got into bed. She seemed to be surprised by her grandmother's appearance. She said to her grandmother, "Grandmother, what big arms you have!"

"All the better to hug you with, my dear," said the wolf.

"Grandmother, what big legs you have!"

"All the better to run with, my dear," said the wolf.

"Grandmother, what big ears you have!"

"All the better to hear with, my dear," said the wolf.

"Grandmother, what big eyes you have!"

"All the better to see with, my dear," said the wolf.

"Grandmother, what big teeth you have!"

"All the better to eat you with, my dear!" said the wolf.

And the wolf gobbled up Little Red Riding Hood.

You're probably wondering where the woodcutter is. In this version of the tale, he isn't.

I never liked the ending where the woodcutter suddenly appeared like Superman and saved the day. Nor did I like the idea of a child being so stupid that she mistakes a wolf for her grandmother.

I loved my grandfather's version of the ending, in which Grandmother is hiding in the closet, and bursts from it with her shotgun in hand. Grandmother then blows off the wolf's ears and tail, and sends him howling and running into the woods. Grandmother and Little Red Riding Hood lived happily ever after in my grandfather's version, and I was very happy with his ending to the adventure.

The source for the version of the story I've shared is Andrew Lang's *The Blue Fairy Book*, 5th edition (London:

Longmans, Green, and Company, 1891), pp. 51-53. The most obvious source for his retelling of the tale is: Charles Perrault, *Histoires ou contes du temps passé, avec des moralités: Contes de ma mère l'Oye* (Paris, 1697). It holds a touch of sexual innuendo, and a harsh, moralistic finale.

There are red riding hoods, red caps, red hats, and naive little girls who get eaten by or saved from the wolf in many folktales from various regions of Europe. On occasion, the girl saves herself and her granny, and kills the wolf. Those were the versions I loved, even with their moral of following the right path and avoiding "the company of wolves."[1]

Old variant's motif:

ATU333, Red Riding Hood

1. An allusion to the work of Angela Carter, which included *The Company of Wolves*, a 1984 British Gothic fantasy-horror film directed by Neil Jordan, and written by Angela Carter and Jordan. The screenplay is adapted from Carter's short story of the same name, as well as her tales, "Wolf-Alice" and "The Werewolf." Angela Carter's stories greatly influenced my ideas of what a good, scary story needed and how a tale could be twisted.

SUGAR

HE USED TO come to the woods every night when he thought his wife was asleep. I don't think she was; I think she didn't care where he was spending his nights, just didn't want to be bothered with him in her bed.

He sent for me when somebody got hurt or sick, slave, cow, even his wife, he sent for me; I was called a healer by everybody on the plantation, got respect from them, too. He just called me "Sugar," told folks, "Go get "Sugar." He didn't want folks to know he was coming to me at night for something besides healing.

Everybody knew. His wife wouldn't let me work in the house, not even in the summer kitchen behind it anymore. I got sent to the fields, to plow and to pick. But he said I was too good at healing, had this cabin built for me far from the house, gave me some seed to plant my own garden. And he brought things for me and the children in those days, sacks of flour, ears of corn, beans or yams, sometimes a ham, sometimes little sugar cakes for his children.

Everybody knew.

Then times got hard with the war and the runaways (God bless every one of them), and him having no sons besides my little ones to help him with the work. Battles in the fields left blood and bodies to fertilize the land. Cattle and supplies were stolen away by the Union soldiers. His wife ran off to her family in New York. He lost everything except the house, and me. I would've run off, too, but my baby girl, his baby girl, was still new to this world, and I wasn't in any condition to run.

One night he came to me, but not the way he used to; he came with the foreman. They left with my three little boys, but not without a fight. Foreman was bleeding from both hands and arms where I'd stabbed him. And that man had a cut from brow to cheek. But they knocked me down, kicked me a few times, threatened to take my baby girl, too, if I didn't stop fighting. I couldn't get up off this floor fast enough to fight anymore. I just lay there and screamed, while my baby girl, swaddled and safe on the bed, screamed the way babies do when they're scared. I screamed, and I prayed, and I cursed, too, until I got up off that floor and held my little girl.

He didn't bring me things anymore after that, left me and the little girl alone. I thought we'd die here when my food supply ran out. Then I prayed that I might be strong enough to keep her from suffering for too long. But I knew I couldn't kill her. We'd have to wait on Death to come.

Then came that blessed night when he didn't come sneaking, didn't come striding, didn't come the way he had to my door. He came running, whispering, fighting for breath, begging, banging against the wood until I thought the door would break.

"Portia, let me in! Let me in! The soldiers are after me!" I opened the door, and he fell into the cabin.

He gasped, "I killed one of 'em. They was takin' the last of my money, last of anything they could carry. That one, he got hold of my spare boots, and I killed him with the fireplace shovel. You have to hide me, Portia. You have to hide me!"

I told him to get in the cedar chest at the foot of the bed. He did.

"What's that sound, Portia? What did I just hear. Did you lock this chest? I didn't know it had a key," he said. His voice was weak, and tired. He was kind of old for all the running he'd just done.

"That was the key turning in the lock, sir," I said. "If the chest is locked, and they can't find the key, well, you'll live a little longer."

"Hide the chest, Portia! Hide me so they can't find me!" Now he was shouting.

I dragged the chest a bit, dragged it to a better spot. I put the big kettle on the hook in the fireplace, made sure not to spill any water as I set it just right; then I stoked the fire and got the awl.

"What's that noise, Portia? What you doin'?" Now he sounded nervous.

"That was the awl, sir," I said, "makin' a hole for you to breathe. "See it? Maybe I better make a few more holes."

"Yes, yes, thank you, Portia, thank you!" Now he sounded

calmer. I drilled a few more holes. The water was boiling.

"What's that noise, Portia? Sounds like somethin' cookin'."

"That's the wind, sir. Storm's coming this way."

"No storm comin', fool woman ... what's that?" Now he sounded angry. "Portia, what you doin?!?"

"That's the rain, sir," I said. "Hot rain, like my tears when you took away my sons."

"Portia, that's hot water! You're burnin' me, you're burnin' me!"

"Yes, sir," I said. "I can't wait anymore for the Devil to do it. I figure you should burn in Hell. But it's takin' too long for you to get there. So I'm just helpin' you along."

He screamed a lot. I didn't want him to wake the baby. And I couldn't keep boiling water and pouring it into those holes. That was too slow. I mustered up all my strength, and dragged that chest to a better spot.

He screamed a lot more, there in the fireplace. He rocked and shook that chest so hard, I thought it would jump out on the hearth. I bundled my baby girl, tied her in her blanket so she settled onto my hip. I went to the wood pile for more firewood, stoked the fire high. He was screaming all the while.

The baby cried, so I sang to her, sang so loud my throat hurt. I tiptoed into the woods when his screams got too loud for me. Took me a while to realize he had stopped screaming, and I was still singing.

The soldiers walked up on me. "Girl," said one of them, "there's smoke comin' from a cabin. That cabin yours?"

"Yes, sir," I said. "A man come through my door, said soldiers were after him. He set the fire to get your attention, and ran off. Now I have no home for me and my baby."

They asked which way he had gone. I pointed. They took off running. One of them told me to walk toward the rising sun, and I would find their camp, and I would be safe.

At sunrise, part of the woods were still ablaze. The wood smelled good, burning like that. The Union soldiers said they had to move the camp; the winds had turned, and the fire was coming in their direction. "But it will eventually burn out," they said. "Easiest thing for us is to get out of its way."

I helped them pack up, with my baby girl smiling and riding on my hip. I promised to cook for them when the new camp was set up.

One of them swore he smelled pig roasting.

"Oh, that's not pig," I laughed. "Pig smells good. That smells a bit rank, too mean to be pig."

The soldier chuckled, "Maybe it's the big bad wolf."

—A NOTE OR TWO FOR YOU—

My version of "The Three Little Pigs" is influenced by stories I've heard and read about the times of African-American captivity before and during the Civil War. Women lost their identities, were given European names, were brutalized, raped, and deprived of their children. Yet many remained hopeful and self-determined, and found ways to survive the times and regain a certain autonomy. This strength of spirit and character should be more than remembered; it should be honored.

The name I chose for my protagonist, "Portia," was

derived from the Latin "Porcia," a feminine form of the old Roman family name "Porcius," which probably was derived from porcus, a pig or hog. I always wondered what really happened to the mother of the three pigs—did she move in with the son who had enough sense to build a house of bricks or stone, or did she die alone. Her character was as important to me as the characterizations of her sons and their nemesis, even when I was a little girl.

The variant that helped me create my version of the story was collected by Emma M. Backus, in her work, "Animal Tales from North Carolina," in *The Journal of American Folklore*, Vol. 11, No. 43 (October-December, 1898), pp. 284-92. This variant was listed as:

How Come the Pigs Can See the Wind

> Did you done hear how come that old Sis Pig can see the wind? Well, to be sure, ain't you never hear that? Well, don't you take noticement, many and many a time, how unrestful and 'stracted like, the pigs is, when the wind blows, and how they squeal, and run this yer way and that yer way, like they's 'stracted?
>
> Well', sah, all dat gwine on is along of the fact that they can see the wind. One time the old sow, she have five little pigs —four black and one white one.
>
> Now old Brer Wolf, he have a mighty good mouth for pig meat, and he go every night and walk round and round Miss Pig's house, but Sis Pig, she have the door lock fast.
>
> One night, he dress up just like he was a man, and

he put a tall hat on he head, and shoes on he foots; he take a sack of corn, and he walk hard, and make a mighty fuss on the brick walk, right up to the door, and he knock loud on the door in a great haste, and Sis Pig, she say, "Who there?"

And Brer Wolf say up, loud and powerful, Brer Wolf did, "Quit your fooling, old woman, I is the master, come for to put my mark on the new pigs; turn 'em loose here lively."

And old Sis Pig, she mighty skeered, but she feared not to turn 'em out; so she crack the door, and turn out the four black pigs, but the little white pig, he am her eyeballs, the little white pig was, and when he turn come, she just shut the door and hold it fast.

And Brer Wolf, he turn down the corn, and just pick up the four little pigs and tote 'em off home; but when they done gone, he mouth hone for the little pig, but Sis Pig, she keep him mighty close. One night Brer Wolf was wandering up and down the woods, and he meet up with old Satan, and he ax Brer Wolf, old Satan did, can he help him, and Brer Wolf he just tell him what on he mind, and old Satan told him to lead on to Miss Pig's house, and he help him out.

So Brer Wolf he lead on, and directly there Sis Pig's house, and old Satan, he 'gin to puff and blow, and puff and blow, till Brer Wolf he that skeered, Brer Wolf is, that he hair fairly stand on end; and Miss Pig she done hear the mighty wind, and the house a-cracking, and they hear her inside down on her knees, just calling on God A'mighty for mercy; but old Satan, he puff and blow, and puff and blow, and the house crack and tremble, and he say, old Satan did, "You hear this yer mighty wind, Sis Pig, but if you look this yer way you can see it."

And Sis Pig, she that skeered, she crack the door and look out, and there she see old Satan's breath, like red smoke, blowing on the house, and from that day the pigs can see the wind, and it look red, the wind look red, sah. How we know that? I tell you how we know that, sah: if anybody miss a pig and take the milk, then they can see the wind, and they done tell it was red.

Old variant's motif:

ATU124, The Three Little Pigs

BLACK ROSES

THE SUN RESTED above the western horizon, and cast a burnt orange glow over the castle. The prince, riding toward it on his noble steed, smiled at his good fortune. Here was his happy ending, the prize foretold in an old fairytale, a tall castle, enclosed in high walls covered with black roses and thorny vines. If he could climb those walls, and enter the castle garden, he would find the princess who had slept for a hundred years.

He left his horse tied to the thick base of one of the vines. His riding gloves were little protection against the black thorns. The scent of the roses, stained the color of dried blood, was nauseatingly sweet. By the time he reached the top of the wall, and let himself down the other side, his head reeled and his stomach churned. But there, in a coffin of glass, like a jewel waiting for his approach, was the princess.

Her skin was as pale as the moon, and so thin over her eyes that he could see the blue of them right through the lids. Her hair was the color of goldenrod and flax, and her lips were almost as dark as the blood-colored roses.

Carefully, he opened the lid. Slowly he kneeled beside the coffin. Swiftly, he pressed his lips against hers.

She sighed, the movement making her thin chest rise and fall. She opened her eyes, looked into his, and smiled. She opened her arms to him.

The prince gently pressed his treasure to his chest. Her heart barely beat, and her breath was cold against his cheek. He smiled, and told her, "It is as the fairytale said. I have come to you, my innocent one, and given you life with love's first kiss."

He felt an excitement that pulsed through him, from his groin to the veins in his neck. His voice sank deeper as he spoke: "I will protect you now; I will keep you close and safe from the world, for now you are mine, and mine forever. The tale is ended."

"My sweet prince," she whispered and smiled, as her lips brushed his cheek, "'tis true. A fairytale brought you here, but it was simply a fairytale. I chose this life; I need no protection against it, or the world.

"And innocence? Is it fairy tale, or merely the delusion of a man that makes you think you were my first?"

He was hypnotized by her voice, so soft, so sickeningly sweet. His heart pounded fast, faster, and the blood rushed through his veins as she sank her small sharp teeth into his neck. The pounding slowed, the heartbeat ceased. The prince released his princess, but she, as strong as the rose vines, held him close. She drained his blood, and dropped his lifeless body to rest and rot among the clean white bones beneath the thorny vines around her resting place.

Ages ago, her story had reached into the candlelight of a tower room. There, beside the dark spinning wheel, the old one had given her the chance for a blessing, or a curse.

"Godchild, a simple prick will seal your fate. Which will you choose—the tip of this spindle that gives you sleep for a hundred years, and youth eternal, or legal bondage to a man who takes your family's throne, your body, and your sovereignty?"

She smiled then, and licked the warm blood that remained on her lips. Better to be herself and sleep a hundred years, than to lose herself, and become a lonely prize upon a pedestal for a prince.

She closed the coffin. She closed her eyes. And Beauty slept again.

Her tale has not yet ended.

—A NOTE OR TWO FOR YOU—

Synopsis of the old tale, as written by Giambattista Basile in his 1634 work, *The Pentamerone*:

SUN, MOON, AND TALIA

Astrologers tell a great lord that the horoscope for his newborn daughter, Talia, reveals that her life will be threatened by a splinter of flax. Talia's father commands that no flax ever be brought into his home. But eventually, young Talia sees an old woman spinning flax, and asks the woman if she might try to do this herself; a splinter of flax is caught under her fingernail, and she collapses. Her father thinks she is dead, but he cannot bear the thought of burying his child. The "body" of Talia is sequestered at one of his country estates.

Time passes. A king, out for a hunt, follows his falcon into the house, and discovers Talia. When he cannot awaken her, he rapes her, then leaves for his own kingdom. In her sleep, Talia gives birth to a boy and a girl. The girl baby, hungry for breast milk, instead begins to suck on Talia's finger; her sucking draws out the flax splinter still embedded beneath Talia's fingernail. Talia awakens, finds her twin babies, names them "Sun" and "Moon," and remains with them in the country house.

Sometime later, the king returns to find Talia alive, awake, and caring for twins. The king wants to marry Talia, but he already has a queen. At home, at night, the queen hears him call out the names of his second family in his sleep. His secretary knows the king's secrets, which the queen bribes and forces the secretary to tell. Then the queen, pretending to be the king, forges an invitation for the twins to be brought to court and tells the cook to kill the children and serve them as a meal for their father. But the cook hides the children and prepares two lambs. And the queen watches and makes sardonic remarks while the king eats.

Then the queen has Talia brought to court to be thrown into the flames of a huge fire. Talia asks if she can first remove her fine clothes. With each garment she removes, Talia screams, and the king hears her cries of grief. The queen tells him that she will burn Talia, and that he has eaten his own children. The king rescues Talia, and commands that his wife, his secretary, and the cook be thrown into the fire. But the cook has saved Sun and Moon, and after a blazing bonfire has gone out, the king marries

Talia, and the cook becomes the royal chamberlain. Everyone lives …

Happily ever after? Horrible! A truly horrid tale on so many levels! And yet, it fostered future retellings and other tales recreated by Charles Perrault, Marie Hassenpflug—the narrator who shared the tale with the Brothers Grimm—and, yes, the Disney studio folks.

Compared to that story, my little vampire tale is a sweet narrative.

Ah, vampires! Their stories have been romantically tidied up, too. Today's versions of the once-nefarious creatures are physically attractive, strangely sexy and excitingly mysterious — they even sparkle, and they have fan clubs! This is a far cry from the frightening fangs, creepy claws and sunken eyes of Nosferatu as depicted by Max Schreck[1], and the dramatically dark eyes and pale flesh of the caped predator Dracula as played by Bela Lugosi.

The tale as shared by Charles Perrault is known as "La Belle au bois dormant," or "The Beauty Sleeping in the Wood." In the tale as share by the Brothers Grimm, the protagonist is "Dornröschen," or "Little Briar Rose." As in many fairytale romances, the reader finds a beautiful princess who succumbs to a spell, and is rescued from her enchantment by a handsome prince.

The version of this tale compiled by the brothers Grimm was a version that had been a previously oral version of the original classic tale published by Charles Perrault in *Histoires ou contes du temps passé* in 1697. This was drawn from *Sun, Moon, and Talia* by Giambattista Basile (published posthumously in 1634), which was in turn coming from one or more folk tales. The earliest known version of the story is *Perceforest*, composed between 1330 and 1344 and first printed in 1528.[2]

According to some folklorists, the story is an allegory for nature's seasonal changes: the natural world is represented by the princess, the wicked fairy or witch or queen represents winter, who causes a kind of hibernation that ends when the prince—representing spring—warmly awakens the sleeping world.[3]

Old variant's motif:

ATU410, The Sleeping Beauty

1. *Nosferatu, eine Symphonie des Grauens* (*Nosferatu: A Symphony of Horror*, better known simply as *Nosferatu*) is a German Expressionist Vampire horror film, directed by F. W. Murnau, released in 1922, and starring Max Schreck as Count Orlok, the vampire.

2. Bottigheimer, Ruth. (2008). "Before Contes du temps passe (1697): Charles Perrault's Griselidis, Souhaits and Peau". *The Romanic Review*, Volume 99, Number 3. pp. 175–189.

3. Lüthi, Max, *Once Upon A Time: On the Nature of Fairy Tales*. (New York: Frederick Ungar, 1970), p. 33.

BY ANOTHER NAME

YOU MIGHT BEGIN this tale with the words, "Once upon a time." They do not always lead to "happily ever after." I sold my soul. That changed my life. Thereby, hangs the tale.

I was bored with the countryside, with the care of my younger brothers, with the life of a country bumpkin unnoticed by those of higher estate. I sought the advice of a dark one, a healer and herb woman who was not as good as her sisters. She sent me to the crossroads at midnight.

I met him there. He appeared first as a shadow, then took the form of a jester playing a mandolin. "A jester?" I questioned, "why not a king?"

He laughed, and the odor of sulfur and brimstone rose from his throat. "My life is a joke," he said. "Mortal, what do you wish?"

"A different life," I immediately replied. "I want excitement, a change from who I am. I want to live for a hundred years, but never want for anything. I want you to curse those boys, my mother's sons, for the life I had to live taking care of them when she and my father died. Take away their good looks; leave them ugly, and small, as my old life was."

"Done," he said. "You know the price?"

It was my turn to laugh. "If there is such a thing as a soul, I have no need for it. My soul is yours, if you give me what I want."

And so it was. I don't remember what happened after that. I remember awakening next to a stream, and hungering for the fish in it. I was so quick, I snatched one from the waters and ate him raw. It was then that I saw myself reflected in the rippling current. I screamed.

And all day long, I cried. At one point, I was chased by a starving wolf who protected her pups. It was then that I found I could tear a wolf apart, and that I hungered for raw flesh and warm blood, and that I could change the shape of a thing merely by running my fingers over it. I changed a fallen leaf to gold, a handful of water to wine, a blackberry into a pearl. But I could not change myself.

I found a cave where I could hide myself. In the back of the cave was a tunnel. It led to deeper caverns of coal. In my anger and woe, I squeezed a piece. It became a diamond.

But what good were diamonds to me, when I was so ugly and small. I, too, was my mother's son.

At midnight, I waited at the crossroads again. He appeared first as a bit of dancing flame, then as the jester again. I told him he had made a mistake, that he had not given me what I requested.

"Is your life exciting now? And are you changed from the man you were? And, like your brothers, your mother's other sons, who will also live a hundred years, you are rumpled and stilted in growth and withered in skin. Ah, that should be your name!"

"I don't want this," I wept and begged, "Please, what must I give you to get back my life, my soul?"

"Another soul, of course, one that is pure, and clean, and new. Bring such a soul to me, and I will return your own."

And so it was that I began to lure the ignorant and innocent to him. Sometimes he made deals with them, too, but none of them were pure enough; in their innocence, they had followed wicked paths, they had already done small, evil deeds. I realized a soul, pure, clean, and new could only lie within a life that had not yet been lived.

It took a hundred years to find a way to get one.

I found a girl with a sad story of her own. Her father had boasted of her ability to spin straw into gold, and sold her into servitude to a king. The king's servants dressed her in fine clothes and a bit of jewelry, and led her to a room filled with straw and a spinning wheel. There, the king pronounced that if she did not make the gold appear by dawn, she would die.

It was easy to creep through a crack in the wall, and appear before her like magic, easy to convince her to give me her diamond ring as I told her I could get the job done. I did the deed. The straw was gold. And she was led to a larger straw-filled room, for the king was greedy.

On the second night, she gave me her pearl necklace.

And on the third and final night of her travail, when there was no fine jewelry to give me, she promised me her firstborn child. A baby, pure, clean, and new, would give me the soul I needed.

She did not expect the child to be a prince. She thought she would go home. The king fancied her, asked her for no more gold, only the treasure of her body. What prices the innocent in this world sometimes pay?

By the time the little prince was born, the king had grown bored with her. I simply walked into her bedchambers and demanded my fee.

She begged and pleaded, no longer an innocent, no longer ignorant. She had not known she would ever conceive, or how much she would truly love her child.

Her tears moved me, not much, but I gave her a chance. "Guess my name. You have three chances to do so. If you do, I will leave and never return."

The first night passed with the guessing of stupid, country names, the second with curious nomenclatures concocted by the ladies in waiting, and the guards, and the cook, all of whom loved this girl.

By the end of that night, I was so sure of my own soul being returned, that I threw myself a party. I ate a bear, tore open his fur coat and devoured his innards. I drank and danced in his blood before a bonfire, I planned to bake what was left of him into a pie, and I sang my joy, and my name.

And the next day?

The third guess. Rumpled, stilted, in withered skin, I heard her call my name. I shrieked, for all was lost to me. I tore at my face, and jumped up and down, until I had made a hole in the earth. My foot stuck there, as, beneath the ground, someone laughed, and the odor of sulfur and brimstone reached my nostrils.

In my rage, I grabbed the leg that was free of the hole, and I ripped myself in two.

Please note that such tantrums resolve nothing. I felt myself drawn beneath the earth. And now, I walk in shadows and fire, and serve my master.

I have made two servants of myself. Sometimes we meet one another. We hug and embrace, and try to pull ourselves together, but never can. Sometimes we simply curse ourselves, for the foolishness at the crossroads.

He laughs, and plays his mandolin, and taps a fine rhythm with his hoof.

And what of the girl? Well, she left the castle, and took her son into the woods. They found the house of my brothers, and moved in, and kept it clean. They never wanted for anything, for my seven brothers, all rumpled, and stilted, and withered in their skins, had found caves where the coal had been squeezed into diamonds.

When the old king died, she became the queen mother, and she and her son did live happily ever after. Time and storytellers emended her adventure into a romance, whose princess had hair as black as night, skin as white as snow, and lips as red as blood.

But that, that is another story, with another name.

—A NOTE OR TWO FOR YOU—

Synopsis of the old tale:

Rumpelstiltskin

A miller bragged that his daughter could spin straw into gold. When the king heard this, he took the girl and locked her in a room where she was to perform her magic. Of course, the girl couldn't actually make gold from straw. A little man appeared and said he would do the magical deed for a price. And he did, twice! But on the third day, the girl had nothing more to pay him, and she promised to give him her firstborn child. The gold was spun. The king married the girl, the two soon had a child, and the girl, now queen, remembered her promise to the little man.

She was heartbroken. The little man gave her a chance to keep her baby. He said the queen must guess his name, and gave her only three days in which to do so. A messenger overheard the little man singing about his name. And when the queen seemed to correctly guess, the little man, enraged at losing what was promised, stomped his foot into the ground and pulled himself in half.

The tale as translated by D. L. Ashliman (© 2002), from Jacob and Wilhelm Grimm's "Rumpelstilzchen," in *Kinder-und Hausmärchen, Vol. 1—Children's and Household Tales* or *Grimms' Fairy Tales* (Göttingen: Verlag der Dieterichschen Buchhandlung, 1857)), ends with these words:

"Is your name perhaps Rumpelstiltskin?"

"The devil told you that! The devil told you that!"

shouted the little man, and with anger he stomped his right foot so hard into the ground that he fell in up to his waist. Then with both hands he took hold of his left foot and ripped himself up the middle in two.

This is a change from an earlier version in the first edition of Kinder-und Hausmärchen, Vol. 1 (Berlin: Realschulbuchhandlung, 1812). The last line of that version states—again, translated by D. L. Ashliman:

"'The devil told you that!' shouted the little man. He ran away angrily, and never came back."

A much simpler, much tamer ending, don't you think?

I love to play with the concepts from more than one tale. Here you may recognize two favorites, "Rumpelstiltskin" and, toward the end of the piece, "Snow White."

Motifs for both the old tale of "Rumpelstiltskin" and my new variant:

ATU500, Rumpelstiltskin (or The Name of the Helper)
H521, The Test, or guessing the unknown person's name
H1092, The Task, or spinning the impossible amount in one night
H513, Guessing with life as a wager

TRAP

I NEVER CONSIDERED the act to be a "murder." And I never hunted. I simply waited. He or she searched me out. I was there, waiting in the darkness. It was time for someone to die.

But the one who approached me this time was not a potential victim. He was a child. He had no business being there in the park, alone as night fell. That was foolish, to be sure, but I couldn't kill him. He was much too young and frail, and the bruises on his pale cheeks and arms clearly spoke of his own dark experiences.

I drew back into the bushes beneath the shadowing trees.

He trudged along the path and over the bridge. With each step, his head slowly turned from side to side; I could tell he was looking for something, or someone. I thought myself well hidden in those bushes. But he saw me. And, instead of being startled or fearful, he smiled, and walked directly to me. His blue eyes seemed to tear up a bit as he looked up at me, yet he smiled.

"Oh, mister," he asked, "I've been looking for you!

"Are you the troll who lives under this bridge?"

He pointed to the stone edifice across which he had walked, eight feet or so away from where we stood. Its solar-paneled lighting system, six antiqued lampposts set in pairs facing one another at both ends and the middle of its parallel stone walls, were glowing like sickened fireflies. Soon, the sunlight would be gone.

I attempted to appear indignant, although the boy's question amused me. I stepped from the bushes. "Troll?" I questioned. You think I'm a troll?"

I knew I had become the stuff of scary tales, a boogeyman who haunted communities near and far. But no newspaper article or television report had ever accused me of living under a bridge or being a creature of fairytales.

In fact, I lived in the penthouse suite of the Willows Hotel just two blocks from this city park. I owned the hotel, along with her sister properties around the world. I was CEO, Controlling Stockholder, Mister, Sir, the face on the cover of a dozen business magazines, the blogger of sound information for success, the entrepreneur, the philanthropist, the subject of television news and interviews, the person other people wanted to meet, or to be. I was Prince Charming, if you will. I'd been called a heartthrob, been compared to Hollywood stars who made hearts flutter and tweets Twitter. And this boy thought I was a troll? How laughable!

But I didn't say that to this boy. And I didn't tell him that, on the third night of every other month, I became Death, at least in my own mind.

It was and is a pleasurable hobby. I'd successfully crafted it and played with it for many years during my journeys from one property to another. I preferred to refer to it as a hobby rather than a habit or obsession. I didn't kill because I felt I must. I killed because it felt right to do so, essential, in fact, to the continuation of an intelligent and worthwhile human race. I could have considered it a calling, no, a ministry.

The modus operando was always the same. It had to be, or the police would not have called my hobby serial killings, would they? I never bothered joggers or lovers or children, or those with an appearance of joy and purpose and an apparent mission in their steps. Near sundown or midnight, depending upon the season and the lighting in the area, I waited for the sluggard to come, alone and desperate for something —money, alcohol, more alcohol, drugs, sex, trespass into someone else's life, anything but what they discovered I offered them in my notes —and, without fail, they read the notes and traipsed to whatever rendezvous I selected. They handed me the notes as proof that they were the persons I'd wanted to meet. They seemed like fish who, when caught, returned the bait to the fisherman.

The next day a body was found strangled with a belt still tightly wrapped around the neck, and the word "SLOTH" printed in red marker on the forehead.

You're probably wondering why I did such things. Not the killings, of course. They are justifiable acts. You're wondering: Why did I label each one a sloth?

Because they were. They spent their lives just hanging around, bemoaning their circumstances without any plan or effort or even willingness to make a change for themselves or a difference for anyone else. Complaining and blaming others for their adult lives was much easier than doing any worthwhile thing. My research informed me that some of the sloths had jobs they hated, some didn't. But they didn't want to work. They seemed to think someone owed them something. I studied the background of each and every one of them. They were sloths.

Why did I use a belt to strangle them? Belts are cheap to purchase, sometimes free. They're neat, usually strong, and fairly easy to acquire anywhere. I could buy them in upscale haberdasheries and middle-class department stores. Those were the places, among many others —expensive restaurants, membership-only spas and golf courses —where I overheard conversations that let me to my future victims. I could also order belts from almost any Internet shopping center, but I didn't like to use credit cards, and I couldn't meet my prey. I had to see and hear the sloths, who hung around their workplaces instead of working, and stole space and opportunities from people who needed and wanted a chance. I performed a civic duty, and improved the economy with my purchases.

I never used the belts in the cities where I bought them. I packed them away for my next journey. A belt from Boston might be used in Honolulu, a belt from Paris might end up in Philadelphia.

And why did I print my victims' true identities in red on their foreheads? Oh, I just like the word, and the color red. Red has a certain flair, and I am a bit melodramatic.

Back to the boy.

"Why would you ask me if I was a troll?" I asked. I glared down, with my nose a bit up in the air.

"Well, sometimes I see you here, and you just stand around the bridge. I thought, maybe, you lived under it.

"I remember the troll lived under the bridge when the three billy goats trip-trapped over it to eat some grass on the other side. And I know the biggest goat head-butted that troll. I ain't never seen any goats around here, so I figure you ate 'em all. And, if you are the troll who lives under this bridge, and you're getting' hungry, maybe you could come to my house and eat my brother."

This conversation was getting interesting.

"Eat ... your ... brother?" I tried not to sound amused.

"Well, he's not really my brother. He says I have to call him "brother." He's my foster mother's son. She's a nice lady, but he's not nice at all; he's real mean. He used to be in jail somewhere, but he came home. And his mother, my foster mother ... her name's Mary ... she wants him to leave. She says he's not supposed to be in her house, that the court says he's not supposed to be there. I think she's scared of him, and she can't make him go anywhere.

"Yesterday he hurt her arm, and he took her grocery money. And today ... this morning ... he hurt her arm again. He hurt me, too.

"Mr. Troll, he probably won't taste as good as a goat. But, if you're hungry enough, he might be okay for you to eat."

I hoped the boy couldn't tell how angry I was. My senses were aroused. I seemed to taste metal. I became aware of the chirping crickets. Somewhere, a cicada, desperate for a mate, made a terrible racket. The noise didn't drown out the sound of an ocean in my head.

I crouched before the boy. His eyes widened. His mouth opened. I took a deep breath and smiled a little. "Boy," I said, and my voice might've seemed a bit troll-ish, "What's your foster brother's name?"

"Buddy," the boy said. He was beginning to fidget.

"How old is Buddy?" I asked.

"Nineteen," the boy shook himself a bit, as if quickly rocking himself for comfort.

I stood. "I can't come to your house. But I'd like to see it. Can you show me where you live?"

The boy sighed in apparent relief, and grinned. "Sure, Mr. Troll!" He reached for my hand. The sensation of being touched was mildly startling, like a low charge of electricity. The boy led me over the bridge to the housing project where he lived.

"Do you wanna know my name, too?" he asked.

"No," I said. "You must never tell a troll your name."

The boy walked me past many old buildings, some in need of minor repairs, some greatly dilapidated and in need of destruction. I reflected on the location and its proximity to my hotel and other downtown businesses. This neighborhood had potential. With some work and other investment, it could be a logical site on which to construct a conference center and hotel complex, and perhaps create an artsy gallery district with a school for disadvantaged students. I was not afraid of investment, or hard work.

The boy and I passed a few bars. He pointed out a very seedy one, Buddy's Watering Hole. I didn't stay long. The boy was waiting for me. When I left the place, I told the boy to walk ahead to his home; I noted the door he entered. I waited across the street, where a few trees struggled to survive. I watched him enter the house.

Soon after, a young man, lean and muscular and slightly tipsy by appearance, entered the same door. He left again within a matter of minutes. He slammed the door behind him. I heard a woman loudly crying behind that door. I listened intently for the cries of a child.

Street lamps now glowed brightly. My prey staggered down the street. I quickly and quietly approached the apartment, and listened. A woman sobbed. A child's voice assured her, "Don't worry, Mary. Everything is gonna be okay. I know it."

I turned and watched Buddy attempt to stagger and swagger at the same time. He paused before that very seedy bar, then lumbered inside, and quickly left again. He headed for the park, my park, my bridge.

I knew Buddy had received the note I paid the bartender to give him. I'd carefully written it with my right hand, as I always did; the handwriting was almost as neat as if I'd written with my left. The note said, "Buddy, meet me at the stone bridge in the park. I have what you need ..."

That note never failed to bring the sloths to me. They anticipated drugs, money, whatever they desired most. Instead, when they met me, I offered them a job at one of my hotels, starting at the bottom and working up from there, provided they were willing to be drug-tested from time to time, and to take some classes I recommended, and to work extremely hard, and keep our meeting and conversation a secret. Occasionally, someone would say "Yes," and I'd have a new and very good employee. But most of the time, I got laughed at, or cursed at, or merely ignored. And I felt for the red marker in one pocket, and pulled the belt from the other.

Buddy was off to the location I'd listed as our meeting place. I wondered what he expected to get.

This time, I didn't wait for my victim to enter the park. This time, I wasn't waiting for a sloth. This time, I was hunting, stalking, I suppose. I walked behind my victim. The belt was in my hand. And I suppose you could say I was as hungry as a troll.

Buddy finally noticed my footfall, quick and closing in on him, too close, too close, and he was too drunk to run. He whimpered when he turned and saw me. He placed his hand on something in his own pocket. But he never drew it into view. He froze. He just stared at me. He didn't speak. But when he saw the look in my eyes, the choked sound he uttered was almost a bleating.

Tomorrow, I leave for one of my other properties. Following Buddy made me break my routine. But I think I liked being a troll. It was a very simple thing to accomplish, and an act of kindness for the world. There are too many people on this planet. Some of them are such lazy creatures that they simply don't deserve to live. And some are downright loathsome.

The boy won't see me again. But, after I've spent some time researching her situation, his foster mother will receive a job offer in the mail. I do hope she takes it.

And now, I must make some plans. There are many parks, and many bridges, and I have a new kind of prey, and a new part to play.

Don't worry. I will never hunt a child. I like them, for they believe in fairytales. Some of them may even turn them from dream-stories to goals, if they are given the chance. No kids, never kids. And waiting for sloths is a thing of the past. I now seek big, bad wolves.

Who's that walking across my bridge? Trip-trap, trip-trap. Trip.

Trap.

—A NOTE OR TWO FOR YOU—

Yes, this is "The Three Billy Goats Gruff," minus a brother, recreated as a contemporary variant. I loved the old tale when I was a child, but I always felt sorry for the troll, who landed on his horns in the stream or river, and either washed downstream or hid himself under the bridge, never to be seen or heard from again.

The idea for my retelling came to me as I remembered a story I overheard, about a new employee who kept calling off from work or not showing up. Actually, the young man's mother would call, to say he wasn't going to be at work because "he wants to go to a party with his friends," or "it's spring break, a long weekend—he shouldn't have to work." I can't imagine asking my mother to call me off from work for anything, especially a party. The young man's "career" lasted less than a month. He sent his mother in to pick up his paycheck, then came in himself to complain that his wages were cut.

Unbelievable.

Synopsis of the old tale:

THE THREE BILLY GOATS GRUFF

Three billy goat brothers want to fatten up on the green grass in the meadow on the other side of a stream. First they must cross a bridge, under which lives a frightful, hungry troll who eats anyone who tries to cross the bridge.

The smallest billy goat starts to cross the bridge, but the troll threatens to gobble him up. The smallest goat tells the troll to wait for his somewhat bigger billy goat brother, who will make a bigger meal. The troll lets the smallest goat cross the bridge.

Along comes the medium-sized goat. He, too, is stopped by the troll and suggests that the troll wait for his brother, who is the biggest of the goats. The troll lets the second billy goat cross and waits for the biggest goat.

The third and biggest billy goat walks onto the bridge. The troll stops him and threatens to eat him, but the biggest billy goat kicks—or butts, depending on the teller's choice—the troll off the bridge and into the stream. The three billy goats eat to their hearts content. The troll is never seen again.

The Norwegian fairytale, "Three Billy Goats Gruff"—"De tre bukkene Bruse"—was collected by Peter Christen Asbjørnsen and Jørgen Moe and first published between 1841 and 1844 in Norske Folkeeventyr.

My favorite version of the tale comes from author Neil

Gaiman, who adapted the story and titled it "Troll Bridge" for an anthology of fairytales retold called *Snow White, Blood Red* (Edited by Ellen Datlow and Terri Windling: EOS, 1993). In Gaiman's short story, the troll wants to eat the life of a young boy who has crossed his bridge. The boy persuades the troll to wait, saying he will return to the bridge after he has lived a little more. The characterizations of child, teenager and middle-aged man take the place of the three goats. The boy, when a man, takes the place of the troll under the bridge; the troll now wears his life, his face and clothes, and leaves the shadows of the bridge for the empty house where the man lived.

Old variant's motif:

ATU122E, eat-me-when-I'm-fatter

MAYBE

GINA PRINCE, DAUGHTER of Buddy "King" Prince, CEO of Royal Industries, was taken into police custody this morning. Prince is accused of the murder of a young man who was a guest in her father's home.

According to servants who were eyewitnesses to the scene, the young man was brought into the Prince home by Gina Prince, after he returned to her a lost prototype for a new product, the Golden Anti-Gravity Sphere. Eyewitnesses said Prince threw the sphere into the air, where it floated for a few seconds, then it dropped into a well on the Prince estate. The young man jumped into the well, retrieved the sphere and asked for a meal as his reward. Eyewitnesses said Prince walked away from the young man, who followed her to the house.

Police Lieutenant John Fricker said Prince claimed the young man who came to her door was a frog at that time, and that he did not become a man until she threw him against a wall. Prince also claimed the young man asked to sleep in her bed.

Prince's father, who invited the young man to join him and his daughter for dinner, would not confirm this.

Police are uncertain as to how such a small woman could have thrown a full-grown man across a room and against a wall, with enough force to break every major bone in his body. Fricker said that police cannot get a statement from Prince, whom this reporter heard repeating, "This is not the way the story is supposed to end. Maybe I should've kissed him." Fricker said that, consequently, Prince will be moved from the police station's holding cells to a hospital for evaluation and observation later this afternoon. Fricker would not say which hospital would be contacted, or when Prince would be transported to it.

At the police station, Buddy Prince refused to answer questions about his daughter, stating, "My Gina seems to be delusional. At the least, she is in a very delicate frame of mind." When asked if the young man was truly a frog when the two first met, Mr. Prince said, "What do you think?"

The identity of the deceased man is still unknown. He was described by Coroner Donald Bland as about 25 years of age, 6'4" tall, 225 pounds, brown-haired and muscular, and wearing tailored attire fit for a king.

The incident is still under investigation.

—A NOTE OR TWO FOR YOU—

Synopsis of the old tale:

The Frog Prince

In the tale originally called "The Frog King"[1] by the Brothers Grimm, a snooty princess unwillingly befriends the Frog Prince—she meets him after he retrieves a gold ball she mistakenly dropped into a pond—who wondrously then becomes a handsome prince. Although in modern versions the change is customarily brought about by the princess kissing the frog, in the original Grimm rendition of the tale, the frog's spell is broken when the princess hurls him against a wall in revulsion. It seems the frog wanted to spend the night sharing the princess' bed: "Now I am tired and want to sleep. Take me to your room, make your bed, so that we can lie in it together. [3]"

Sounds like psychological manipulation to me.

In other early versions it was sufficient for the frog to spend the night resting on the princess's pillow.[4] But, this story, in any version, wasn't a favorite of mine. It spoke of abuse in many forms: the princess is too snobbish, or too judgmental of his appearance, to want to keep her promise that the frog can come and dine with her; the king is a supporter of loyalty at any cost, but seems negligent of his daughter's safety when he says she must let a stranger come into her bedchamber and sleep; the frog is demanding and annoying, and it's possible that he will remain that way when he is a prince. Where's the love in all of this?

Maybe the witch who enchanted the prince and turned him into a frog knew exactly what she was doing.

Old variant's motif:

ATU440, The Frog Kin

1. Jacob and Wilhelm Grimm, "Der Froschkönig oder der eiserne Heinrich," *Kinder- und Hausmärchen, 1st ed., Vol. 1* (Berlin: In der Realschulbuchhandlung, 1812), No. 1, pp. 1-5.

2. Annotations for "Frog King". http://www.surlalunefairytales.com/frogking/notes.html#EIGHT

3. Frog Kings. http://www.pitt.edu/~dash/frog.html

4. *German Popular Stories*, translated [by Edgar Taylor] from the Kinder und Haus Märchen, collected by M. M. Grimm, from Oral Tradition (London: C. Baldwyn, 1823), pp. 205-210.

SILVER AND GOLD

ASPASIA WAS A good girl, and the fairy blessed her for that. Each time she opened her lips to speak, coins of silver and gold fell from her mouth. And all who saw Aspasia vomiting money thought, how fortunate she is. She will never want for anything.

She, however, had other thoughts, all beginning with "How can I ...?" How can I know that the one I love loves in return, when he or she dotes on my mouth, raves for my lips, writes odes to my tongue, and never looks into my eyes? How can I be sure our relationship is good, that our love is true, when my spewed income is the only reason for conversations each and every day? How can I enjoy a meal, when each bite is tinged with the taste of metal? How can I whisper words of love, sigh after a kiss, exclaim at the heights of passion, knowing that my lover is keeping a bucket ready nearby?

Once Aspasia had sneezed during an intimate moment, and nearly put out a lover's eye. And he picked up the coin, looked at it with the eye that could still see, and said, "Thank you!"

After a while, Aspasia grew silent, and hid herself in a chamber of her castle —why would she continue to live in a hovel when she could afford the very best? Still, she sometimes wished for a hovel shared with someone who truly cared about her. Her parents were dead. There were no lovers. There were only attendants, servants, counselors, and guards, tenant farmers and their families, musicians, artists, and poets, all of whom Aspasia subsidized in some way. She wrote interrogative or declarative notes to all of them, depending on what was wanted or needed. She spoke to none of them and ate alone. At night, she sat in her gilded rocking chair and sang herself a lullaby. Her tears sparkled like diamonds, and the coins she spewed glistened in her lap, and at her feet.

Then Aspasia went to bed, alone, on a feather mattress covered with soft pillows and silken sheets. Sometimes she dreamed. Sometimes she snored. She choked herself awake on the bits of gold that caught in her throat.

Finally, desperate for this cursed blessing to end, Aspasia sent two of her guards to search for the fairy who had touched her lips with treasure. Her note to them read:

You will find the fairy near the farm where I worked for Livia and her mother. Sit near the gate, place a small bowl of milk on the path that leads to the door, and listen for something that sounds like a mewling kitten. At sunset, the fairy will come for the milk. You will know she is the right one by her long nose and the glow of her yellow eyes. Catch her carefully as she drinks the milk, and put her in the bag I've given you. Tie it tightly shut, and bring it to me.

I caution you, DO NOT MAKE A WISH, AND DO NOT ACCEPT ANY GIFT THE FAIRY OFFERS. The consequences may be dire. They will definitely not be what you expect.

Three months passed before the guards returned. One of them was wearing a pair of donkey's ears in place of the ones he'd worn at birth. The other pursed his lips, as if they held a secret.

Aspasia sat at her desk. In a quickly scribbled note, Aspasia asked the one who pursed his lips, "Did you make a wish?"

He nodded. He sighed, and a dozen toadstools plopped from his open mouth onto Aspasia's rich carpet.

Aspasia hugged each of them. She carefully took the bag from the one with donkey ears. She wrote another note, sending both of them to the kitchen. She heard a pot or pan clatter to the tiled kitchen floor. She heard the cook scream, "Donkey ears?!?"

Aspasia locked and bolted her chamber door. She checked the windows to make sure they were locked, too. Then she set the bag on her desk, and carefully opened it.

"Ah, it's you!" buzzed the fairy. "In need of another wish, dearie?" The fairy laughed a snorting laugh. Snot ran from her long nose.

Aspasia nodded. She didn't dare speak. She wondered if the fairy could read a note.

"No need to write a note, girl," the fairy said. "I know what you want.

"Mind you, if I take away your gift, you'll eventually be a poor one again. You'll not have enough to live in this fine place, nor to pay servants to wash your pretty gowns and fine sheets.

You'll end up leaving all of this behind. You'll be as poor as you were when you worked for Livia and her mother.

"Are you sure you want that?"

Aspasia nodded. She fell on her knees and clasped her hands tightly together. She couldn't resist saying, amid a spring of money that trickled from her tongue, "Please!"

The fairy sighed. She walked over to Aspasia, and patted her knee. Then she bit the knee, a bite that hurt worse than any insect's sting.

Aspasia yelled, "Ouch!

And that was all that fell from her mouth.

She would have thanked the fairy, but the little creature was flying toward a locked window. Quickly, Aspasia ran to open it. Out into the night flew the fairy.

She hovered, her yellow eyes glowing like tiny fireflies. "Shall I visit Livia then?" she asked. "Do you think she's tired of spewing worms and frogs?"

"Oh, yes, do visit Livia, please," said Aspasia, and she meant it. Even though Livia had been too lazy to do the chores her mother set as Aspasia's tasks (for which Aspasia had never been paid, only beaten), even though Livia had refused to do the work the fairy demanded in order to receive "a gift," she didn't deserve a mouthful of horrors each and every day.

Aspasia imagined Livia eating, sleeping, the taste of Livia's weeping. Horrors!

Aspasia never heard from Livia and her mother, even though she was sure they knew she still lived in her palace. She never had to consider a move. She had stored so much fairy treasure that she, and eventually a loving husband, and eventually their children, lived a very pleasant life, as did all who lived with them on Aspasia's vast and prosperous estate.

The fairy was never seen again.

But when her children were old enough to ask for fairy tales, Aspasia found herself thinking about Livia and her mother. Aspasia told them a story of two women who took in an orphan, and beat her and made her do all the work and live like Cinderella, until a fairy with a long nose and yellow eyes came to the gate where the poor girl sat and cried. The fairy asked the girl for a saucer of milk, and said, "If you will come and work for me, I will give you an odd and wondrous gift."

Aspasia ended the story with the words, "When the lazy girl demanded a gift, even though she'd refused to do the fairy's housework, the fairy touched her lips, and she grew back to her normal size, but worms and frogs fell from her mouth.

"But each time the good girl spoke, gold and silver coins fell from her lips." Aspasia's husband smiled, and her children marveled, "Ah. How wonderful!"

Aspasia turned her head to hide a single tear. It sparkled like a diamond, but thank goodness, it was only a tear.

One day Aspasia sent messengers to the old farmhouse, with an invitation for Livia and her mother to come and visit. She thought they might be grateful that the worms and frogs had stopped crawling and hopping out of Livia. She wanted them to see how happy she was.

She sent a note, even though she could safely speak:

All is forgiven. Come feast with us, and tell me how you

fared once the fairy's curse was lifted.

Three months passed. The guards returned with a story of their own. Neighbors claimed that, many years before, they heard Livia and her mother screaming and arguing with one another about whether to leave a bowl of milk beside the gate, or beg for someone or something to return. The neighbors, who were never welcome on Livia's mother's farm, hadn't gone to see what happened and assumed the two had been fighting over a cat. The noise went on for more than a day. Then there was silence.

Weeds filled the gardens. The cows broke through their fencing and roamed freely in the pastures; they lowed to be milked, so a few folks got up the nerve to take them back to their barn, to milk them and feed them properly, and to go to the farmhouse. The stench of something dead greeted them as they approached the farmhouse door.

The neighbors found two women buried beneath a mound of silver and gold. Their mouths were filled with coins.

—A NOTE OR TWO FOR YOU—

Synopsis of the old tale—the variant known as "Diamonds and Toads":

DIAMONDS AND TOADS

An evil-tempered old widow had two daughters, an older one who resembled and was just as mean and prideful as her mother, and a younger daughter, who was as sweet, kind, and beautiful as her late father had been.

One day, when the younger daughter was drawing water

from the family's well, an old woman appeared and asked for a drink. The kind girl gave water to the old woman, who was really a fairy disguised as a crone; the fairy had taken on this appearance so that she could test mortal beings and discover the character of their hearts. Because she had been kind to the fairy, the girl was given a blessing: whenever she spoke, a flower or a diamond or some precious stone would fall from her mouth.

The kind girl got home late, and tried to explain what had happened. Her mother's anger turned to delight when she saw the treasure that fell from her daughter's lips. She wanted her favorite child to gain such a blessing; after instructing the mean daughter to be kind to any begging crone she might meet, the woman sent her mean daughter to the well.

But this time, the fairy appeared as a princess who asked for a drink from the well. The unkind elder daughter was rude and insulting, and refused to draw water for the disguised fairy. As punishment for the mean girl's attitude and actions, the fairy proclaimed that, each time the girl spoke, a toad or a snake would fall from her mouth.

When the mean girl arrived at her home, she told her mother what had happened. With every word, a horrible toad or a slithering snake fell from her mouth. Enraged by the favorite daughter's misfortune, the cruel widow threw her kind younger daughter out of the house.

The kind girl wandered in the wood. There, she met a prince, who immediately fell in love with her. They were married and lived happily.

Eventually, the cruel widow could no longer tolerate

the disgusting creatures that fell from the older daughter's lips. The widow made the older daughter leave. The mean, older girl remained in her miserable state. She died alone in the woods.

This variant can be found in Andrew Lang's *The Blue Fairy Book*, under the title "Toads and Diamonds."

As a child, I loved to hear a story that I remember as "For Pete's Sake." Each time the kind young girl discovered something strange, she remarked, "For Pete's sake!" This is how I remember it:

A young girl sought her fortune, in order to be of help to her poor and sickly family. She ended up working for a mean woman and her lazy daughter. When she received one penny for a long day's work, the young girl made a wish (or said a prayer) that she could quickly make enough money to go back home and help her family.

That night, she slept on the hearth, keeping warm by the fire (a very "Cinderella-ish" moment). Early in the morning, the young girl heard something in the pasture. She went outside and discovered a strange cow mooing for someone to milk her: "For Pete's sake," the cow said, "somebody better milk me! I'm about to explode!" The girl obliged the poor cow, and the cow disappeared.

As the young girl carried two buckets of milk toward the back door, she saw an apple tree appear right in front of her. Overloaded with fruit, the tree begged for someone to pick some of the apples: "For Pete's sake," the apple tree said, "Somebody better pick some of these apples! I'm about to fall over!" The young girl set a ladder against the trunk of the tree, and a bushel basket beneath it. She picked as many apples as she could and dropped them into the basket. When the young girl climbed down the ladder, the tree disappeared.

Then the young girl heard a noise in the oven. There, a pan of cornbread begged to be removed before it burned. Using the edges of her apron as oven mitts, the young girl carefully removed the cornbread from the oven and set it on the table. She waited for the cornbread to disappear.

That's when she heard some little feet pitter-pattering around the corner of the house. The young girl stepped outside and stood on the backdoor stoop. A little man appeared; he ran toward the young girl. In each hand, the little man carried a sack ("toted two croaker sacks" was the way I really heard it told).

Seeing this man no taller than her kneecap, the astonished young girl asked, "Well, for Pete's sake, who are you?" The little man yelled, "For Pete's sake, I'm Pete!" He threw the bag at the girl and disappeared around the side of the house. The young girl fell, but when she sat up, she found gold and silver coins stuck to her apron, and more coins falling out of the two sacks.

The young girl left some money on the kitchen table for the mean woman, stating that the woman might be able to pay a better wage for someone to work for her. As the young girl left, the mean woman asked where she got the money. The young girl told her story, and went home to her family.

The mean woman was greedy enough to tell her lazy

daughter that she must get up early the next morning and look for a strange cow, a strange apple tree, and a strange pan of cornbread. Because there was a promise of fortune, the lazy girl agreed. But each time the lazy girl had an encounter with one of those oddities, she said something rude —"You might as well explode, then; I'm not milkin' ya!" "You'd better go ahead and fall over, 'cause I'm not pickin' any apples!" "Well, burn up, then! I'm not takin' ya out of the oven!" —and refused to work. She didn't milk the cow, or pick any apples, or remove the cornbread from the oven. Her chances for good fortune disappeared.

Then the lazy girl heard those little feet. And she, too, met Pete, who threw two sacks at her before he disappeared around the side of the house. From the bags, as well as from the lazy girl's apron pockets, toads and frogs leaped and hopped, and eels and worms slithered. The lazy girl and her mean mother got no treasure beyond the coins that the kind young girl had left on the table.

Many of the protagonists in my family's stories had simple names or no names at all. They were called "that little girl" or "the old woman" or "a silly boy" or "ornery old man" or "Rabbit" or "Turtle." Occasionally, the main characters bore the names of "Janie" or Jack" or "Simon," even "Jack Sprat."

The names I chose for my protagonist and antagonist in "Silver and Gold" were "Aspasia" and "Livia." Aspasia is derived from Greek and can mean "welcome one." "Livia" is derived from Latin and can mean "blue" or "envious." Both are strong names that felt oppositional to me.

When I read “Toads and Diamonds,” I saw no blessing in what the fairy gave to either the kind or the unkind girl. Stuff falling from your mouth did not seem like a good thing, even if the stuff was diamonds and flowers. Diamonds might cut the tongue; flowers might gag the throat. Never mind the reaction to honking up toads.

Thus, you have my version of the story.

Old variant’s motif:

ATU480, the kind and the unkind girls

WHAT DO YOU DO?

WHAT DO YOU do when you wake up, alone in the dark, and realize that someone is breaking into your house?

Forest didn't like the sounds he heard downstairs. They were unfamiliar thumps and bumps, whispers that sounded like voices coming through a hollow pipe, occasional giggles and snickers, buzzings and hummings and clicks. Forest was supposed to be alone, in his Uncle Frank's bedroom, in his Uncle Frank's bed, in his Uncle Frank's silk pajamas, in the house he had inherited from his Uncle Frank.

No one had really broken in. There was simply the jingling of keys, then the clicking of the lock on the huge wooden door, the door creaking open, and, then, those sounds. How many people were there?

Forest reached for the phone on the nightstand. He couldn't reach it, no, he couldn't find it. Had he knocked it on the floor as he rolled around filled with dreams, and alcohol?

Maybe he could find a weapon? No. Forest knew every

nook and cranny of his Uncle Frank's room, all its secrets, all its hiding places, where his uncle had hidden money, mementos of dalliances and trysts, and good, strong liquor from his aunt. But no guns. They were locked downstairs in the gun cabinet in Uncle Frank's study.

Forest slid off the bed, tiptoed to the door, and opened it. It squeaked with a high-pitched squeal.

Downstairs, a woman's voice said, "Listen, did you hear that?"

"I did," said a man's deep voice. Then I tenor male voice chuckled and said, "Cool."

Forest held his breath. They were coming toward the stairs, at least three people coming to rob the place, and maybe kill anyone they came upon in their robbery. They stopped at the bottom of the stairs. Forest didn't dare try to close the squeaky door.

"Frank. Frank Warren, is that you?"

The voices began to whisper again. The footsteps headed toward the back of the house. The softer male voice called out, "Frank Warren, are you here?" Then the footsteps trailed off somewhere in the vast expanses of the first floor.

Maybe Forest could get to the study downstairs, and grab a gun, and call the police. They probably wouldn't come, since they'd already been at the house that evening to tell Forest that the case would now remain open as an unsolved murder.

Better to just get a gun, one of the rifles, so that he wouldn't have to get to close to anyone. Forest would be within his rights to shoot the strangers that were traipsing around in his, his house. He could kill them, and get away with it. Even if they had a key, they had broken in.

Forest lifted the door a bit as he opened it by its doorknob, just enough to keep it from making any noise. Then he tiptoed down the hall, and softly scampered down the stairs.

At the bottom of the stairs, Forest unconsciously stepped over the place where Aunt Miriam had landed when she fell. He got into the study without making any noise, and slowly closed its door behind him. The door, warped with moisture and age, wouldn't close completely. Forest quickly headed for the big mahogany desk, and pulled at the top drawer.

It was empty, no gun cabinet keys, no keys at all, no papers, nothing. Had the thieves already been in here at some time? Is that how they got the key to the front door?

I'll just have to break the glass in the door, Forest thought, and hope I don't cut myself. But there were no guns in the gun closet, and the glass was gone. Now Forest really wanted to call the police. Those intruders must've already taken Uncle Frank's guns!

And they were coming back. They stopped near the study door.

One man shuffled around, and asked, "Tell me about this guy again?"

"He died in 1956, the result of accidentally drinking poison. An overdose of medicine prescribed for his heart trouble and his depression, to be exact. It was all stirred into a bottle of brandy."

Ah, thought Forest, they know what I did to Uncle Frank.

But if they know he's dead, why do they keep calling his name?

"Accidentally drinking poison? If he deliberately drank the stuff, wouldn't that be suicide?"

Of course, thought Forest. Everybody knew Uncle Frank was alone, deeply saddened by the unexpected death of his wife, on the verge of a nervous breakdown and struggling with irregular heartbeats, and taking drugs for both. Uncle Frank had told the neighbors that he didn't want to live, had told the minister to prepare a sermon for his funeral, had stopped eating, bathing, dressing, or letting anyone into the house.

Except me, thought Forest. Except me, his favorite nephew. And I had keys to every door, including his liquor cabinet. And I had mixed the medicine into the brandy, knowing that Uncle Frank would drink whatever I gave him. And I had handed the bottle to him with gardening gloves on my hands, and the excuse that I was finally going to pull up that old, dead bush near the kitchen door. And I had locked the doors behind me as Uncle Frank had gagged and lurched to the floor and had very slowly gone to sleep forever.

I had locked the doors and quietly walked away just as I did on the night I pushed Aunt Miriam down the stairs.

"Miriam Warren, is that you?" The woman was asking questions again. Apparently, they didn't know Aunt Miriam was dead. Maybe they thought she'd survived the fall.

"Frank or Miriam, we're not here to cause any trouble. We just want to see you," said the man with the deep voice.

Forest laughed softly.

"Did you hear that?" asked the softer male voice. "That

wasn't an EVP. I could hear it with my own ears! He's here!"

EVP? What's EVP? What did they hear? Forest hadn't heard anything strange except for the noises these intruders were making, and his own laughter.

The door creaked just a little as Forest tried to close it a bit more.

The young woman squealed and touched her cheek. "I think I heard something move," she whimpered.

"If you're here, show yourself!" the deep voice shouted into the darkness. "Forest Warren, if you're here, give us another sign!"

Forest stood very still, held his breath, prayed that these crazy people would go away. If they didn't hear anything else, perhaps they would leave.

"Forest Warren!" the man shouted again, "Did you mean to kill yourself?"

Oh, thought Forest, he has the wrong name. He means Frank Warren, but I'm not saying anything.

"Forest Warren, do you feel guilt or remorse? Did you mean to drink the brandy you'd poisoned for your uncle to drink? Did you plan to kill yourself after murdering your aunt and uncle, or did you just drink from the wrong bottle?"

The wrong bottle? The ... what was this idiot talking about? Drink from the wrong bottle?

"Mr. Warren, are you sorry for what you did? We know you thought you got away with the murders. It's the year 2012. Nowadays, forensics evidence would've given police more clues, and you probably would've gone to jail," said the young woman.

"If you hadn't drunk the poisoned brandy, you might've gotten away with the crimes. Forest Warren, do you feel guilty about all of that?"

A memory crept back into Forest's mind, slowly, tickling at his thoughts, tickling like a spider working on her web. The memory was of one word, spoken as Forest toasted his inheritance, his good fortune, with brandy poured from a snifter he'd put back in the secret liquor cabinet in Uncle Frank's bedroom, because he'd forgotten to get rid of it before he locked the doors.

The police had come, seen the pill bottle and the spoon and the glass, and assumed that Uncle Frank had mixed his own fatal nightcap. They'd gone over every inch of Uncle Frank's study, but they hadn't even looked in his bedroom; after all, the man had died in his study. And when they'd gone, Forest sighed with relief, and dragged his drunken self, dressed in his Uncle Frank's pajamas, back upstairs to his Uncle Frank's bedroom, where he'd opened the secret cabinet, and grabbed a bottle, and poured himself a drink, and gulped it ...

... the memory was of Forest's last word as he tasted the bitterness in the glass, just one word:

Oops ...

Forest fell to the floor and screamed. The ghost hunters heard a loud banging sound, as if something, or someone, had fallen to the floor. They tried to run into the study, but something slammed the door. All the doors slammed then, and the three intrepid investigators ran to the front door, and pulled it open, and ran, giggling and laughing and squealing like little girls. The young woman shouted, "I got it! I got the voice as it screamed!"

They stopped talking and listened to a small bit of electrical equipment. Forest's scream, a bit of electronic voice phenomena, was just an anguished whisper after the sound of something falling to the floor.

Forest cried and cried until the sun began to rise. Then the ghost hunters gathered up all their belongings, and made sure the house was tidy and secure, and locked the huge front door with the key on the key ring they'd received from the local historical society.

They exchanged high fives and fist bumps as they loaded their van and agreed: "Haunted. Definitely haunted. Cool."

Well, what do you do when you know you're dead? When you know what you did to others, and what you did to yourself? When you realize that the fortune is gone, and the grand house is a wreck, that your time has come and gone, and you have lost everything, including your life?

Forest went upstairs, and went back to bed. Forest thought, this bed probably isn't even here, but I am. Then Forest settled himself into his uncle's bed, pulled up the covers, closed his eyes, and prayed, earnestly prayed, for the first time in his life, or death.

Forest prayed that he would go to sleep, and never wake up again.

—A NOTE OR TWO FOR YOU—

Synopsis of the old version of the story:

Rip Van Winkle

Rip Van Winkle lives in a village by the Catskill Mountains. He is an easygoing fellow, and much loved by the villagers, but he is henpecked by his nagging wife both day and night.

One day Rip goes hunting in the mountains, where he meets and drinks with the crew of English explorer Henry Hudson. He falls asleep, and awakens twenty years later. When he returns to his village, Rip discovers that he has slept through the Revolutionary War. King George no longer rules; George Washington works for the good of a new nation. Rip's gun and his faithful dog are gone.

Everything has changed, including his marital status. His nagging wife is dead. But Rip is eventually identified by his daughter and son, and is accepted by the villagers as a somewhat eccentric old man.

Did you see my connections to Rip Van Winkle in this story? Well, that's the seed-story for it. Consider the protagonist in both: a drunkard, who sleeps away a lifetime. Good ol' Rip might've been a better person than Forest, but they both fell into an adventure, and a kind of sleep, thanks to a taste for liquor.

Sometimes tearing a story down to its simplest notions, then analyzing a single notion —in this case, one aspect of the character's personality —are all that is needed to spark a different concept for the plot.

Although "Rip Van Winkle" is the original character and work of Washington Irving, it, too, is rooted in older tales, including the classic story of many European fairytale collections, wherein a man helps the fairies and is freed of his life's torments and advanced into a time and place where he will be respected for his age and admired and supported by his loving children or villagers. Some examples:

The Jewish Talmudic story of Honi M'agel, who falls asleep for 70 years. When he awakens, he finds that he has a grandson, but nobody believes that he is Honi. He prays to God, who takes him away from this world.

The story of "The Seven Sleepers of Ephesus," in which a group of early Christians (about 250 A.D.) hide themselves in a cave, in order to escape persecution during the reign of the Roman emperor Decius. They fall into a deep sleep and awaken 200 years later during the reign of Theodosius II; the city of Ephesus and the whole Roman Empire have become Christian. This Christian story is recounted in a Sura of the Koran, known as Sura Al-Kahf.

In Orkney, an archipelago of Northern Scotland, a folktale tells of a drunken fiddler who, on his way home, hears music coming from the burial mound of Salt Knowe near the Ring of Brodgar. This fiddler finds his way into the mound, where the trolls are having a party. The fiddler stays with the trolls and makes music for them; he plays for what he believes is a span of two hours. When he gets home to Stenness, he discovers that fifty years have passed. This tale may very well be one source for Washington Irving's retelling, since Irving's father, an Orcadian from the island of Shapinsay, probably knew the tale.

Old variant's motif:

ATU766, sleeping hero legends

A motif for my version of the tale:

E175, death thought sleep

A GAME OF CARDS

ONCE THERE WAS a man named Lucius, who spent his nights card-playing and carousing at the local house of ill repute. Lucius was married to a goodhearted woman by the name of Laura Lee. She was as good and God-fearing as Lucius was awful and devil-may-care.

Laura Lee never fussed or complained. But she hid her sewing and baking money, which she used to keep the house standing and the icebox full. And she prayed over Lucius whenever he spent a little time at home (usually just long enough to eat, sleep, and change his underwear), but nobody in the community understood why. All that praying did was annoy him, and encourage folks at church to pray for his wife.

Laura Lee prayed for herself, too, but it sounded like more of a conversation than a prayer: "Lord, you know I feel like an idiot for having married Lucius. I expect it was my way of getting' away from my Mama. But I could'a just gone to live with Great-Aunt Mary and Great-Uncle Charlie. Would'a been easier takin' care of them in their ol' age than it is dealin' with Lucius every day.

"Lord, I know matrimony is a sacred institution, and I ain't askin' you to unbind the ties that hold us together. But I sure would appreciate it if you stretched 'em just a little, maybe take Lucius off somewhere so that he don't come home again. If you won't do that, then I ask for your strength to get through each day. And I'm thankin' you in advance for whatever you choose to do. Now I think I'll make myself some tea."

That was the way Laura Lee prayed for herself. When she prayed for Lucius, she kept her hands folded and her eyes closed. She stayed far away from him while he ate or slept, and her mouth moved but nobody but the Good Lord heard what she said.

Still, whatever Laura Lee was saying made Lucius itch. He'd threaten to kill her. He'd storm out the door. Laura Lee would just stand by the cookstove. Something was always cooking on that stove.

One day Lucius jumped up from the table as if to knock Laura Lee to the floor. He never knew she could move that quickly until that moment. By the time he rose, Laura Lee was holding the pot she heated up every morning. Lucius realized the pot's contents were grits. Those grits were hot. The pot was steaming.

Lucius also realized that Laura Lee hadn't been making grits every day because she liked eating them all the time; a pot of hot grits thrown with good aim stuck to the skin and burned a body badly. It was something every woman who'd ever married a man like Lucius could learn from a North Carolina auntie, like

Laura Lee's Great-Aunt Mary.

Lucius lost his itch. He slowly sat down again, and picked up the ear of corn he'd been gnawing while Laura Lee prayed over him. But he stopped himself from taking a bite, and said,

"Laura Lee, what do I have to do to get you to stop tryin' t'convert me into a good man? I like bein' the man I am. It suits me."

"Well, Lucius," Laura Lee said. She still held the pot in her potholder-protected hands. "Well, you could leave."

Lucius laughed. "Now why would I do that? You take real good care o' me. And I know that somewhere around here, you've got some money hidden away. When my luck runs out, you always give me some of that money. I guess you always will. You won't always be standin' near a pot o' grits."

Laura Lee tried not to cry. She could feel her whole body shaking as she said, "Well, Lucius, if you won't leave, maybe you could pray sometime? I know somewhere in you is the young man I met not that long ago. That man used to pray with me. Lucius, will you pray?"

Lucius laughed so hard that he almost choked. Then he threw the corn cob across the room. It hit the wall and slid to the floor. Lucius stood up and turned to Laura Lee.

"Oh, yes ma'am, I'll pray. I'll pray for luck in my card-playin'. I'll pray for a pretty woman to sit on my knee while I pray."

"Oh, Lucius, please, don't pray like that," Laura Lee's voice trembled. "The Lord will hear you, and the Devil, too."

"Let 'em hear me! Let 'em hear. Let the Good Lord send

the Devil to me on Sunday. I don't care!

"In fact, let it be this Sunday mornin'! Let the Devil show up in his finest suit, with a deck of cards in his hand. And my only prayer will be that I take all his money, or go to Hell tryin'!"

Laura Lee gasped. She set down the pot and ran out the front door. She didn't come back, not for her clothes, or her pots and pans, or her money. She ran to her mama's house, and her mama hugged her close, and said she was glad to see her, and talked with her all through that night. Then Laura Lee's Mama helped her buy a train ticket to go to North Carolina and visit her Great-Aunt Mary and Great-Uncle Charlie.

In the meantime, Lucius went on a rampage. He tore up the kitchen and the parlor and the bedroom, tore everything out of the cupboards and the closet, and he found Laura Lee's measly savings in the box where she kept her Bible. Lucius took all of it with him to his card game that night.

He lost every penny.

That was on a Friday. About noon on Saturday, Lucius dragged himself home. He remembered Laura Lee was gone when he walked in and saw the mess he'd made. He ate the rest of the dinner she'd made for him. Then he drank the liquor he'd kept hidden in the tool shed, hidden against more of Laura Lee's praying. He wondered why he'd ever married that woman.

Lucius awoke at the kitchen table on Sunday morning. He was stiff and sore from sitting in a hard-backed chair all night. His right cheek and hair were soaked from drool and slobber, and his mouth tasted like somebody had stuck a dead cat in it. Lucius sat up and smacked his lips. Then he stopped, and stiffened.

Sitting across from him was a man in a tatty red suit. At least, it looked like a suit, but it was hard to tell where it ended and the man himself began. He was red, too, clean up to his hairline, where a crop of shocking white tresses steamed like the grits in that pot on Friday night.

His ears were pointed, his teeth were pointed, and the tip of a tail that waved behind him was pointed, too. Lucius cautiously bent to look under the table for what he expected to see, whether he wanted to see it or not. And there it was, polished like ebony, shining like the patent-leather shoe on the stranger's other foot.

A cloven hoof.

The Devil grinned, and the air crackled and sizzled like frying bacon. He breathed in, and the room went cold. He breathed out, and Lucius smelled sulfur.

The man lifted up his arm and slammed something down on the table. Lucius, afraid to take his eyes off the one who sat and grinned at him, glanced quickly at the deck of cards set before him.

The Devil picked up the cards, and shuffled them seven times. Then he set them down again and shoved them toward Lucius.

"It's Sunday mornin', Lucius, and I'm ready to play poker," the Devil said. "Deal 'em up."

Weeks later, Laura Lee got word from one of the folks at her church that her house had burned down and all the contents of the structure were gone. The letter also said she shouldn't worry about Lucius; it seemed that no one was in the house at the time. Folks thought Lucius had burned the place and run off. According to the police reports, he hadn't been seen by anyone since the morning after he'd visited one of those bawdy houses he so enjoyed.

Laura Lee's mother wrote to her, too. Her letter said the rubble and ashes of the house smelled of sulfur. The letter also stated that the house, which Laura Lee's mother had owned, was insured, and the money would be enough to build a new home.

But when Laura Lee got herself back to see the remains of the place where she'd tried to make a home for herself and Lucius, she told her mama not to rebuild there. The land smelled like burnt bacon and rotten eggs, and that stink wouldn't go away. Neither would the playing cards that seemed to reappear every time somebody tried to remove the rubble. On the back of each one was a red devil with a wide grin and a shock of white hair.

Laura Lee made her home with Great-Aunt Mary and Great-Uncle Charlie. She loved them and took wondrous care of them until they died. They left her their house, and all that was in it, as well as a bunch of stocks and bonds nobody knew they had. Laura Lee ended up sitting in the catbird seat for life.

She still went to church every Sunday. The rest of the week Laura Lee kept talking to God, thanking Him and carrying on those conversations. And every now and then, the conversation included:

"Well, now, Lord, this is nice, this is nice. If this ain't my happy endin', I'd say it comes pretty close."

—A NOTE OR TWO FOR YOU—

Synopsis of a similar story.[1]

According to a tale from Dorset, England, several young men gathered on a Sunday in a secret location (a barn) to drink and play a game of cards —drinking alcohol and card-playing were considered a sin on any day, but especially on a Sunday! A stranger dressed in fine clothing and with the bearing of a nobleman, entered the barn and asked to join the game. Thinking they might win a large amount of money from this apparently wealthy man, the young men invited the stranger into the game.

When it was the stranger's turn to shuffle the cards, he dropped one. One of the other players bent down to pick it up, and saw that it was the four of clubs, which is known as "the Devil's bedpost." That player also noticed the stranger's black, cloven hoof. He screamed to the others, who smelled the aroma of brimstone in the air. All the young men knew who the stranger was. They ran for their lives, and never returned to the barn or their card-playing again.

The same incident is said to have occurred in Maynooth, Ireland. But in that retelling, the sacred time is Lent, the dropped card is the ace of spades, and the stranger who joins the card game is dressed in black right down to his hooves.[2]

My grandfather, Byard Wilmer Arkward, also told the tale, in a version from the Appalachian/Affrilachian (African-American Appalachian) region that included the "Deal 'em up" statement I use in my retelling. His storytelling influenced my written tale.

Old variant's motif:

N4, gambling with the devil

C12.5.12, man swears he can beat the devil in card playing—devil appears, is detected by his hoofs

1. Source: "Gambling with the Devil," www.darkdorset.co.uk/-with-the-devil. Information there comes from a compilation of folklore and stories, *Dark Dorset: Tales of Mystery, Wonder and Terror*, by Robert J. Newland and Mark J. North (cfz, 2007). The tale is said to have occurred around the mid-seventeenth century, at French Mill Lane, near Shaftesbury.

2. Source: "The Devil and Irish Folklore," an article posted on March 31, 2014, by Roisin at http://randomdescent.wordpress.com

MARY STELLA

MARY STELLA WAS a strange child.

Tom Grody knew that as soon as he saw her, skipping and singing as she moved into the house next door with her mother and her father.

Mary Stella was very small, too young to go to school, thought Tom Grody. Her face was round, with large, pale gray eyes. Her frizzy, corn-shock yellow hair framed her face like a dandelion top about to blow away. She wiggle-waved slim fingers at Tom Grody, and skipped back and forth as she carried little items into the house.

As her father and mother removed boxes and crates from their truck, Mary Stella filled a little red wagon with items of apparent importance to her: a faded blanket, a couple stuffed toys, and a tea set, all of which she placed in the wagon with great care.

Then Mary Stella yanked the wagon's handle. The wagon wheels struggled into motion on the uneven grass. Mary Stella pulled her treasures along the side of the house, across the back yard, down the alley behind the houses, into the ancient cemetery behind the long-abandoned church. In the cemetery, Mary Stella looked closely at the markers and monuments she passed. She finally stopping in front of a simple marble gravestone.

Tom Grody watched her every move as Mary Stella removed the treasures in her wagon. She spread and smoothed the blanket over the grave in front of its gravestone. Then she placed each of her dolls on two sides of the blanket. They sat crookedly, a rag doll and a one-eyed teddy bear.

Next, Mary Stella set out the items for tea, a toy teapot in the middle of the blanket, and teacups and tiny spoons on saucers, one setting for the rag doll, one for the one-eyed teddy bear, one for some guest not yet in attendance, and one for Mary Stella.

Mary Stella pretended to pour tea for each of her guests. Then she sat at her place and rocked herself as she sang some sing-song lullaby.

Tom Grody shook his head and went to introduce himself to the parents. He was certain that Mary Stella was a strange child.

Weeks passed. The neighbors seemed neighborly enough. They greeted Tom Grody whenever they saw him, and occasionally invited him to sit with them and chat on their front porch. Sometimes the mother gave Tom Grody cookies or a slice of pie to take home with him. Sometimes Mary Stella stopped her playing long enough to stare at him. Then she gathered her tea party into the little red wagon, and headed for the cemetery. As he chatted with her parents, he would hear Mary Stella singing: la la, la la, la la la-la la ...

During the work week, Tom Grody was always up before the sun. He got himself ready for his foreman's job at the steel mill, packed his lunchbox, and left his house as the sky was changing from deep blue to sunrise's teal and gray. One morning, as Tom Grody walked toward his truck, he saw Mary Stella standing beside it. In the streetlamp's glow, she looked more like spirit and shadow than a child.

She was barefooted and wild-haired, dressed in a white nightgown and holding the paw of her one-eyed teddy bear. She looked up at him with those pale eyes, and quietly asked, "Mr. Tom Grody, did you kill your wife?"

Tom Grody felt the blood wash from his head and body down to his feet. He swallowed a few times before he tried to speak. "Wha-what? Why would you ask me such a question? Who ...?"

Tom Grody stopped himself from talking. He straightened himself to his full height, stepped past Mary Stella and got into his truck. He tossed his lunchbox onto the passenger seat, and quickly started the motor. He didn't wait for the truck to warm up, as he usually did. When he pulled out of his driveway, Mary Stella was still standing there.

Tom Grody's truck screeched around the corner and juddered up the long hill past the empty church and the houses of sleeping neighbors. He parked in his usual parking place at the mill, and realized he'd been holding his breath most of the drive to work. He exhaled, inhaled slowly, exhaled again, grabbed his lunchbox, and slammed the car door as he headed to his locker. He threw the lunchbox into the locker, and trudged to his machines.

At lunchtime, he forgot to eat. Instead, he walked back and forth beside his truck, occasionally pressing his fist against its side. When the whistle sounded at the end of his shift, Tom Grody was so agitated that he practically ran to his truck. It screeched and rattled as he turned into his driveway, shut off the engine, slammed the door. He didn't go into his own house; Tom Grody headed next door, where Mary Stella's parents sipped sweet tea as they sat on the front porch steps and watched the sun go down.

Tom Grody told them what their child had said to him, a grieving widower whose wife had been buried just a few months ago. He panted as he spoke in quick, short sentences: Her accident was tragic. No one was sure what happened. He had found her. She died so young. Cruel people were still guessing and gossiping. Otherwise, why would their child ask him such a horrid question?

And why was she up so early, and outside, all by herself?

Mary Stella's mother and father stood and apologized. "Mr. Grody, we didn't know anything about your wife," Mary Stella's father said. "We don't know many of the neighbors yet. We keep pretty much to ourselves. We'd never gossip about such a thing, but we didn't know about it, until you told us just now." He looked at his wife for affirmation.

She took his hand, and nodded. "It's Mary Stella," she said. "It's just the way she is. She ... sees things. Hears things. She does and says things, sometimes, that we don't understand. See, Mr. Grody, Mary Stella was born with a caul over her face. That gives some folks visions and powers. And, well, she's the first-born daughter of the seventh daughter of a seventh son, and that could make a person kind of strange, too, I guess.

"We're sorry, Mr. Grody," Mary Stella's mother continued. "We'll talk to her."

Tom Grody's breathing had relaxed as he listened. He could hear Mary Stella, singing her song in the cemetery.

"Oh, that's alright," he said. "I'm sorry, too. I shouldn't have let myself get so upset. I guess my heart is still tender about the whole thing.

"Don't worry about talkin' to Mary Stella," he said. "I can hear her in the cemetery. I'll go have a little talk with her myself. Don't you worry, I'm not mad anymore."

Tom Grody did his best to smile a calm and reassuring smile. As Mary Stella's parents walked back onto the porch, he headed along the side of the house, across the back yard, down the alley behind the houses, into the ancient cemetery behind the long-abandoned church.

Mary Stella and her dolls were having tea again. Her head was down as she rocked herself and sang her la-la lullaby song.

Tom Grody crouched beside her. He put his hand on her shoulder. Mary Stella kept rocking. She didn't look at him.

Tom Grody said, "Mary Stella, this morning you asked me a question. What was it you asked me?"

Without looking up, Mary Stella said, "I asked you if you killed your wife."

Tom Grody slowly inhaled. He asked, "Why did you ask me that question? Who told you to ask me that question?"

Mary Stella stopped rocking. She said, "Your wife."

Tom Grody felt himself shaking. He looked at the gravestone behind the child. His grip tightened on Mary Stella's frail shoulder.

"Mary Stella, what's my wife's name?" he asked.

Mary Stella said, "Margaret."

Tom Grody got on his knees on the blanket in front of Mary Stella. "Well, I guess I'll answer your question now, Mary Stella," he said, and the words seemed to sizzle on his lips.

"Yes, I killed my wife. I broke Margaret's neck, and threw her down the stairs. Everyone thought she'd had an accident. And they'll keep thinking that, unless somebody tells them otherwise.

"I killed my wife, Mary Stella," Tom Grody's face was close to hers now. "And, somebody soon, I'm gonna kill you, too."

Mary Stella sighed. She shook her head. "No, Mr. Tom Grody," she said. Her voice seemed deeper, not childlike at all. "No," she repeated. "No, you won't."

And Mary Stella looked at Tom Grody, not with the pale gray eyes he knew, but with the dark brown eyes of his dead wife, Margaret.

Tom Grody jumped up, tripped as he stepped off the blanket. He couldn't seem to move any farther. He couldn't run. He couldn't scream. He just watched that body with Margaret's eyes as it stretched, and grew into the figure of a woman, Margaret's figure, with Margaret's long black hair.

As Margaret walked toward him, he saw Mary Stella, the real Mary Stella, step from behind Margaret's gravestone. The child watched as Margaret smoothed the black hair at her forehead, and pulled it away. The hair, the face, the skin, the flesh, the muscle and sinew of Margaret slipped from the bones and slid downward in a soft, wet puddle at her feet. Margaret stepped out of the puddle. Her bony fingers reached for Tom Grody.

Her right hand touched the right side of his neck. Her left hand grasped his left shoulder. There was a twist and a yank ... the body of Tom Grody fell to its knees, and the head dropped, bounced a few times, rolled, and came to rest at the feet of Mary Stella.

Margaret turned toward the little girl. She seemed to float toward her. Then Margaret's mouth opened, and from the skeletal jaws came a whisper, "Thank you."

Then Margaret seemed to shimmer like water touched by the setting sun's light. All that was left of her spun into a sprinkle of firefly light that danced toward the rising moon and disappeared.

Mary Stella looked into the gaping, silent mouth and wide-open eyes of Tom Grody.

He looked a bit surprised.

Mary Stella folded her arms and glared at him. "I tried to tell you, Mr. Tom Grody," she chastised him. "I was gonna tell you this morning. I knew you killed your wife. She told me. Margaret told me.

"And, Mr. Tom Grody, you know what else Margaret told

me? She told me she was gonna rip yer head off!"

Mary Stella grasped the hair on Tom Grody's head and set him down in the empty place at her tea party. Then she sat and poured tea for her guests, and rocked and sang her la-la lullaby song.

Mary Stella was a strange child.

—A NOTE OR TWO FOR YOU—

Synopsis of a similar tale, heard when I was a teenager:

The Pond

A man grew tired of his wife. He drowned her in a spring on their property. He dug a shallow grave at the edge of the pond that the spring fed, then dug a good bit more and in such a way that the pond would overtake and cover the grave.

A few days later, the man reported his wife missing. Everyone knew they didn't get along, and it was easy to assume that she'd left him. The man avoided the spring for quite a while, but eventually he decided that, if the body was found, folks would think his wife had drowned. So he went down to the spring, to loosen dirt at the gravesite, and let his wife's body rise in the pond.

As he approached the pond with his shovel in hand, he heard a woman's voice. At first the woman cried, then she screamed, and a wind rushed at the man. He dropped the shovel and ran toward his home, but the wind blew so hard that it stopped his forward progression. When he turned, the wind blew in his face from that direction. Then he thought he saw someone walking toward him from the pond, and he heard that someone crying and screaming again. She was running at him, but now she didn't look like his wife. Now, she was a thing of ragged flesh and bones.

The man ran for the sheriff, and admitted what he had done. His wife's body was found, and the man went to prison. He went insane, and died in an institution. And nobody ever bought his house, or spent time near his property. It was said that at night, folks heard a woman cry or scream. And, sometimes, they saw her rising from the pond, walking toward them and reaching out with bony hands.

I have no source for that story, just a memory of a bunch of teenagers sitting on my family's front porch, and telling stories to scare the bejeebers out of one another. I know the teller wasn't a family member. If he or she had been, the "spring" would've been a "crik."

A similar story can be found on pages 19-22 in the wonderful collection, The Telltale Lilac Bush and Other West Virginia Ghost Tales, by Ruth Ann Musick (1965, The University Press of Kentucky). It's called "The Tragedy at the Spring" (tale #13).

As for the mention of the caul and the offspring being the firstborn of the seventh daughter of a seventh son, that's old family folklore. A caul is amniotic membrane that is usually easily removable at birth. It may cover the baby's head, or head and face, and sometimes the entire body. If a child was born with the caul unbroken and covering his or her face, that child was said to be protected from evil, and very lucky.

Being born as a seventh son (or daughter) or the offspring of such a "blessed child" was said to make one "charmed" or "blessed"; this child could be or become a healer, and could have the gift of "sight" of the past, the future, and the supernatural. Some folks claimed that such children might be the Devil's own (that wasn't a belief in my family). Or they might become werewolves.

Old variant's motif:

E221, dead spouse's malevolent return

E230, return from dead to inflict punishment

CAMPFIRE TALES

THIS WAS THE first campfire of summer camp, the first late-night gathering for a rowdy group whose experience in the woods at night would be enhanced by the first roasted marshmallows of summer, the first S'mores, the first camp sing-along, and the first ghost stories. Swinging long sticks and making lots of noise, the young campers marched down the long, winding dirt trail to the place where log seating and a low fire waited for them.

Their camp's mentors walked in front of them and at the end of the line. The camp director wondered if the park ranger who was meant to be their storyteller would arrive soon. Patience did not seem to be a virtue of these campers.

A park ranger was already waiting behind the fire. He stood in full uniform, with his wide-brimmed hat low over his face. He stood next to the storytelling stump upon which camp storytellers sat to share their narratives. He nodded at the campers and their mentors, who sat on the logs around the fire. The camp director led songs about bugs and bears and boa constrictors. Then everyone except the park ranger began roasting marshmallows on those long sticks. They burned some of them, and dropped more of them into the flames than they managed to squeeze between graham crackers and soft squares of chocolate. The park ranger stood, and never said a word.

With full mouths and sticky fingers, the campers turned toward the storytelling stump. They expected the park ranger to sit or stand on it, the way the director and some of the camp mentors did to make announcements. But the park ranger continued to stand. He raised his head just a bit, so that his voice could be heard over the din of excited voices of the campers, who waited for something scary to begin:

"I'm not scared of ghost stories. They're never really scary." "Maybe he'll make 'em really creepy. I like really creepy stories!" "Oh, I hope they're not too scary. If they're really scary, I might pee on myself." "Ew! That's disgusting!" "Yeah, that's worse than a ghost story! Don't sit next to me, if you think you're gonna pee!" "Shut up!"

The park ranger said, "We'll start with a story that's not too scary." And he began the first tale of the evening:

"It was that night when children dress in strange costumes, and run from house to house to ask for tricks or treats. Suddenly a woman appeared before one trick-or-treater. She gazed into the eyes of that one and held up one long, thin finger as she asked, 'Do you know what I can do with my long fingernails and my ruby-red lips?'

"The trick-or-treater screamed and turned and ran away

as quickly as he could.

"The woman walked through the darkness until she came upon another child, and asked, 'Do you know what I can do with my long fingernails and my ruby-red lips?'

"That child screamed as the first child had, and dropped her bag of treats. Crying and screaming, she ran for home.

"And the woman walked on. She came upon another child. Again, the woman asked, 'Do you know what I can do with my long fingernails and my ruby-red lips?' This time, the child was too afraid to run away. He stood there, too frightened to run, too frightened to scream.

"The woman held up one hand, curled one long fingernail toward her ruby red lips, flipped the fingernail against her lower lip, and said ...

The park ranger rubbed his own finger against his lips to make a silly sound, "Bu-bu-bu-bu-bubba."

No one spoke. A few campers snickered. So did some of their mentors. Then one camper slowly and audibly inhaled; she commented, "That ... is the dumbest thing ... I ever heard." And more comments from other campers followed that one.

"Aw, I know that story. Is that as scary as you can get?" "I don't know," said another, "That woman was kinda scary." "No, she wasn't," said another. "She was just stupid. That story was stupid!" "Yeah," another agreed. "Stupid! That wasn't scary at all!"

The park ranger didn't look up from the fire. He simply said, "It wasn't meant to be." Then he touched the brim of his hat, and began another story:

"The very next day, while the children were at school,

a strange man walked through the neighborhood. He walked slowly, with his shoulders hunched forward, and his eyes glared at every house. Then he walked toward one of the houses and knocked on the door —thump, thump, thump.

"A woman opened that door. She was startled at the man's appearance. She asked him,

'W-who are you?'

"The man grinned a wide, toothless grin, and replied, "I ... am ... the ... VIPER!"

"The woman slammed her door. And the man walked to another house, where the same thing happened.

"Every time someone opened the door, the man said, 'I ... am ... the ... VIPER!' And another frightened neighbor slammed a door in his face.

"Finally, there was only one house left, only one door the strange man hadn't approached. He stood on the sidewalk, grinning that toothless grin, rocking back and forth, shuffling his feet. Then he walked to the door and knocked—thump, thump, thump.

"The door was opened to him, and again he said, 'I ... am ... the ... VIPER!' The woman at that house tried to slam the front door, too. But the strange man knew what might happen this time. He grabbed the doorknob, and held the door open. He grinned his wide, toothless grin, and, at last, he could continue with what he had to say:

"I'm the vindow viper. Ya vant any vindows vashed?"

A few snickers were heard again. But the comments began immediately:

"That wasn't scary, either," said one of the campers. "That was just stupid! You're not a very good storyteller." "Well, it was a little scary. I almost peed a little." "You're a little scary. Quit talking about pee. Move over!" "Shut up!" "You shut up. That wasn't scary at all!"

The park ranger said, "It wasn't meant to be." He began another story:

"One night, a young couple drove out to the place in the woods where lovers would meet in those days. It was quiet, secluded, invisible from the road. They stayed there a long while, doing what young lovers do (Here, there was a snicker, and a whispered "Shut up!").

"Then they decided it was time to go home. But the car wouldn't start. The young man, excited about his date, had forgotten to fill the gas tank. He told his girlfriend that he would get the gas can from the trunk, and run up to the road that led to the highway.

"'We passed a gas station to get here. If I run, I can be back in no time,' he said.

"'No!' his girlfriend grabbed his arm. 'Don't leave me here! Don't you remember what we heard on the news? That a mad killer escaped from the penitentiary near here? Let me come with you. Don't leave me waiting here!'

"The young man explained, 'I can run a lot faster than you. If you come with me, you'll just slow me down. Lock the doors. Leave the windows open just a crack. You'll be okay. And I'll be back before you know it.'

"He smiled to reassure her. Then he closed the driver's

side door, and watched his nervous girlfriend. Lock the doors and open the windows just a crack.

"The young woman watched her boyfriend run toward the road. She folded her arms tightly, as if to hug herself. She couldn't tell how much time had passed. The woods were quiet, except for a breeze that grew from a whisper to a shushing of leaves and rustling of branches. Something scratched rhythmically at the roof of the car. A dangling branch, the young woman thought, a branch broken by the wind.

"The young woman listened to the sound. Somehow, it was soothing to her. She peered into the darkness outside the passenger side window, then the driver's side, then the rear windows, then the side mirrors, then the rearview mirror. Eventually, she closed her eyes. She prayed for her boyfriend to quickly return ...

"The young woman opened her eyes to sunlight, scarlet red and golden, breaking through the trees. The sun was rising, and her boyfriend hadn't returned. What had happened to him?

"The young woman opened her car door. She would walk home, she thought. She headed for the road, then remembered that she hadn't closed that car door. She turned, she saw ...

"Her boyfriend was hanging upside-down from a tree branch. His dead fingers brushed against the roof of the car, as he slowly swung back and forth, back and forth, back and ..."

"Woo! Okay, that was scary!!!" "Too scary! I think I peed my pants!" "Ack! You are disgusting! Get away from me!" "Shut up, shut up, shut UP! This is getting GOOD!" "I think I want to go back to the cabins. I think I'm ready to go now. I think I ..." "No! I want to hear another story! We're finally getting' to the good stuff! You got another story?" The park ranger smiled, and lifted his chin, just a little. "Oh, yes," he said, "I have another story. I saved the best one for last.

The park ranger sat on the storyteller's stump, and began his last story:

"Last year, someone did escape from the institution for the criminally insane that was built far from the city, but very near this park. The man was a murderer; he had committed horrible crimes. And he killed two guards in his escape.

"The criminal somehow managed to climb over the walls of the institution, then ran into the woods. It's easy to get lost in these woods, and that's what happened to him. It got dark, and, even though the month was June, the beginning of summer, the evening air grew chilly.

"The killer saw a fire, built right here, in the fire pit at this circle of logs. The killer saw a park ranger standing beside the fire. The park ranger was waiting for his very first group of campers to come down that path, and sit on these logs, and face the storyteller's stump, where the park ranger would sit to tell stories.

"The park ranger heard someone coming through the woods. He turned on his flashlight, and pointed it toward the stand of trees. The killer walked toward him and demanded his uniform and hat. The young park ranger refused to give up the uniform he'd worked so hard to wear. It was a badge of honor for him.

"The killer yanked the flashlight from the park ranger's

hands. He knocked him to the ground; the ranger's hat fell from the young man's head. The killer beat that young man with his own flashlight, pounded his head in with it, until the skull was broken, and the park ranger was dead.

"That's when the killer heard voices on the trail. The campers were coming for their stories. The killer ran, taking with him the park ranger's flashlight. He ran deeper into the woods.

"Did I tell you that it's easy to get lost in these woods? Yes? Well, even with the flashlight, the killer couldn't find a road. Eventually, the flashlight grew dim, and went out. And the killer was never found. Some say his body was ravished by wind and weather and hungry wild creatures, and his bones still lie somewhere in these woods.

"The young park ranger was buried with honors, wearing the uniform for which he had fought, for he was an honorable man. But his work had remained unfinished. That storytelling time around this campfire was his very first call to duty. He hadn't fulfilled his duties; his work was left undone.

"And so, he comes to the storyteller's stump, to wait for the campers to come down that trail, to gather around the campfire and roast their marshmallows and laugh and sing, before he tells them stories.

"He keeps his hat low on his head, so that no one can see the marks, the blood, the cracks left on his skull by his own flashlight. But when he begins his last story, the park ranger removes his hat ... "

The park ranger slowly lifted the brim of his hat from his forehead. But no one saw. All the campers were screaming, running back up the trail to their cabins, followed by their camp leaders, mentors who didn't want to hear the end of the story any more than their campers did.

One of the adults turned as she ran, and shouted at the park ranger, "That story is very, very scary, entirely too scary!"

The park ranger removed his hat. He scratched at the wounds covered with bloodied hair, at the bruises and cracks and holes in his head. Then he set the hat carefully back in place. As the flames dwindled and their light faded, so did he.

"Very, very scary?" The park ranger smiled, then he sighed, "Yes, that was very scary.

"It was meant to be."

—A NOTE OR TWO FOR YOU—

Silly spookers and urban legends are a staple of campfire storytelling. I wanted to share a few with you. Putting them into one story was a challenge to myself. I think it worked pretty well.

The silly stories I've included in this story are: the ghost with the long fingernails and ruby red lips; the "Viper." The urban legends I've used in this story are: "The Hook" or "Hookman" or "The Murderous Madman" or "Boyfriend Goes to Get Gas"—these are only a few of the titles given to these classic motifs for the serial-killer type urban legends.

Synopsis of "The Hook":

A young couple parks in a lovers' lane area. As they hug and kiss—the tale from the 1950s and 1960s is pretty innocent—the car radio blasts a new report: a serial killer has escaped from a nearby institution. He is extremely dangerous, particularly because a metal hook replaces one of his hands. The young couple hears a scratching sound on one of the car doors, and quickly speed away. When they get to the young woman's home, her young man walks around the car to open her door (a mannerly behavior, proof that he is a good kid), and discovers a hook hanging from the door handle.

Synopsis of "The Murderous Madman":

A young couple parks in a lovers' lane—or the woods, or on a dirt road in the country. The young man leaves the car, because he must walk to a gas station and fill the gas can in order for them to get home—or because the car has broken down and he must get someone to help, or because he has to relieve himself. The girl waits in the car, and eventually turns on the radio to pass the time. She hears about an escaped mental patient or serial killer. She turns off the radio, and hears a scraping or thudding sound on the roof of the car. After a while, she gets up the nerve to open the car door, and sees her boyfriend's mangled body hanging from a tree, with the fingers of one hand scraping against the car roof—or she sees the killer sitting on the car's roof, bumping her boyfriend's head against it. This one does not end well for either the young woman or the young man, no matter how good they seem to be.

I reviewed the stories, which I already knew from campfires and midnight storytelling sessions with fellow Girl Scouts, by going to en.wikipedia.org/wiki/The_Hook and www.urbanlegends-myths.com/thehook/murdererwithahook.html.

A wonderful source for the silly spooky jokes, such as the

"Long Fingernails and Ruby Red Lips," "The Viper" formula tales, and the creepy "boyfriend goes to get gas" story variants, is The James T. Callow Folklore Archive. It is a part of the folklore archive of the UDM (University of Detroit Mercy) McNichols Campus Library, which includes traditions gathered by students between 1964 and 1993, as well as the Peabody field note collection of approximately 12,000 folklore entries from Tennessee and the Southeastern USA.

The online Folklore Archive is searchable by text, title, keyword, location, subject and Boggs number (Ralph Steele Boggs, internationally renowned folklorist, 1813-1982). Its subjects include urban legends, ethnic jokes, songs from fraternities, sororities, scouts, drinking games, graffiti, initiation pranks, superstitions, gestures, riddles, proverbs, customs, festivals and elder lore: http://research.udmercy.edu/find/special_collections/digital/cfa/index.php.

OTHER IDEAS: GAMES I PLAY

TO PASS THE time on long layovers or flights or doctor's waiting-room appointments, or to give myself a swift kick in the ol' imagination, or just for the fun of it, I sometimes play mind games that throw odd characters, folktale plots, and silly or scary stuff together. The results of some of these games have, at times, become useful stories. At other times, they have become snickers and chuckles that I tried to disguise as throat-clearing or coughing spells in public places.

In this day and age, folks rarely pay attention; often, they are wired up, tuned in, tuning out, taking selfies, and taking naps. There are times when I do the same—except for taking selfies—tried it once, looked like a drunk jack-o'lantern. But I like playing my mind games more than reading from my Kindle library or checking my emails. Once, in a world—airport—where obnoxious people could become fairytale witches, the obnoxious woman who was loudly chastising her silent husband became the witch in the gingerbread house. With one push, into the oven —an airport automatic waste disposal unit—she went, and her husband enjoyed hearing her bubble and burst. I came back to reality, and found the husband asleep with a contented look on his face, and the wife gone! I got a little nervous, until the wife returned with two tall, aromatically caffeinated drinks acquired on a journey to Starbuck's.

I have shared some of these games in high-school and college classrooms and in storytelling and story-writing playshops. I thought you might like to play a few of them.

See what stories you can create from these four exercises. If you play them as mind games while you're sitting in the airport, learn to pretend that you are clearing your throat, reading your Kindle, or taking a nap.

EXERCISE 1
GODZILLA MEETS CINDERELLA: CHARACTERS AND CHARACTERIZATIONS

Object of the game:

Create a story that results from the personalities and meeting-point of two disparate characters.

Materials needed:

- "Airport" version—your ability to imagine characters from stories, books, movies, plays, television shows, life, anywhere, and throw two of them into one story.
- Group-participation version for two or more players—a set of at least twenty character cards. Create your own, or use the forty-two characters from my list. Add six blank cards for players' own character ideas.

CHARACTER CARDS

Alien	Fairy Godmother	Red Riding Hood
Angelic Child	Frankenstein's Monster	Rumpelstiltskin
Angry Spouse	Giant	Sinister Librarian
Baby Monster	Godzilla	Sleeping Beauty
Bad Fairy	Goldilocks	Snow White
Batman	Granny	Spider/Anansi
Big Bad Wolf	Hansel and Gretel	Three Bears
Big Foot	Henny Penny	Three Billy Goats
Chicken Little	Hare/Rabbit	Three Pigs
Cinderella	Jack	Tortoise/Turtle
Crazed Storyteller	Loch Ness Monster	Troll
Doctor Who[1]	Patient Parent/ Mentor	Vampire
Dracula	Prince Charming	Werewolf
Dragon	Rapunzel	Zombie

1. For those who are not Whovians, Doctor Who is a traveler in time and relative dimensions in space, in a series originated in the United Kingdom when I was a kid. It is still going, and The Doctor (as he is called) has reincarnated many times—different actors with different personality traits for the protagonist—in a contemporary fantasy that has reached iconic heights. If that's too much strangeness[2] for you, consider using the hero of H.G. Wells' *The Time Machine*, who is known only as the "Time Traveller" in the work as it was originally published in 1895.

2. I don't think there can be too much strangeness for you. After all, you are

reading this book.

- Tools for writing or recording your ideas, if you want to keep them.

How to play:

A player selects two characters, considers their personality traits, and how they might react to meeting one another in any folktale or fairy tale or contemporary movie/play/television story. The player then creates a synoptic version of this story and shares it with other players. The game ends when all the cards have been used, people get tired of playing, or your plane lands. In classrooms—grades 5-adult classes—this is a great exercise in creative writing, as well as on opportunity for critical thinking and debates over the logic and reasoning in characters' responses and actions toward one another.

EXERCISE 2

IN A WORLD WHERE ... ACTIONS AND OUTCOMES

Object of the game:

Creative, logical, and critical thinking!

Materials needed:

- Imagination, an understanding of narrative process —beginning, middle, and end.
- Tools for writing or recording your ideas, if you want to keep them.
- The list given below, plus your own ideas.
  - Every pond holds one frog who is an enchanted prince. As a potential monarch, what do you do?— Note: in this scenario, a player might be the one

considering finding the frog, or the player might be the frog.

- Every home is a castle with a tower. As the new owner of such a home, with strange noises in your tower and no key to open its door, what do you do?
- Cookies can come to life. As the owner of a bakery with an order for ten dozen gingerbread men, what do you do?
- Everyone is a pig, and Big Bad Wolves run the housing industry, which mandates that all new houses be made of twigs or straw. As a potential home-builder, what do you do?
- The giant's widow has pressed charges of robbery and murder against Jack. As Jack's defense attorney, what do you do?
- Fairies, giants, trolls, gnomes, and dragons exist, and they have all moved into an apartment complex in your community. As the new manager of that complex, what do you do?
- An old woman is a goddess, and her old man is a god, but they have both forgotten who they are. They still have great powers. As their nurse, what do you do?
- Everyone wears glass slippers. Concerned for the next day's work schedule, your blind date runs away from you at midnight, but leaves behind a distinctive glass slipper. You realize you never asked for a name, don't have an address, don't have an email address; you only have the contact number sent to you by the

dating service, and the dating service does not reply to your requests for more information. As a lovelorn romantic with a glass slipper in hand, what do you do?

How to Play:

A problem has already been stated. You must come up with the solution, and the resolution to the narrative. This game usually leads to some lengthy discussion, or a sense of time travel when you realize you have boarded your flight, made your journey, and are landing in another city.

Exercise 3
There's a Place: Settings

Object of the game:

Enrich one's telling or writing of a story by becoming aware of the setting, and how that setting may impact the story's narrative path.

Materials needed:

- "Airport" version—your ability to imagine the settings of your favorite stories. I will concentrate on folk and fairy tales in this example.
- Group-participation version for two or more players—a set of at least ten story titles. The stories must be known to all players. If they aren't, begin the game by telling short versions of the stories. Create your own list, or use the following twelve folktales rooted in European storytelling traditions:

Folktale Set

Chicken Little	Cinderella	Henny Penny
Jack and the Bean-stalk	Rapunzel	Red Riding Hood
Rumpelstiltskin	Snow White	Three Bears
Three Billy Goats Gruff	Three Little Pigs	Tortoise and Hare

NOTE: This is not a particularly multicultural list. When I use this exercise in classrooms—grades 3-adult classes—the teacher and I have already introduced the students to folktales from around the world, and the list includes diverse tales from several countries or regions such as: Anansi the Spider from Ghana and the West Indies, Ajapa the Tortoise from Nigeria, Momotaro, or "Peach Boy" from Japan, La Llorona, or "The Weeping Woman from Mexico, or tales of Hare and Rabbit in variants from around the world, etc. Thus, the game's participants can research several geographical and socio-political areas in order to describe a story's setting.

- Tools for writing or recording your lists, if you want to keep them.

How to play:

This game works well as an exercise for individuals or teams—I suggest no more than three people on each team. In one minute, participants list every detail they can relate about the setting of one scene in one story

Examples:

- The Little Pig's House of sticks
- The Tower room in Rapunzel's story
- The place in the forest where Chicken Little gets conked by an acorn

The player with the longest list of details wins the round; the player with the shortest list is eliminated. Usually there are three rounds, with stories and settings agreed upon by the players before the game begins. Through the process of eliminating the shortest list each round, somebody wins. If you're playing the airport version of the game, you always win!

EXERCISE 4

THE THING IS ... DETAILS, OBJECTS AND PLOT POINTS

Object of the game:

Recognition of minor details, significant objects, and necessary plot points required for a story to effectively be told, written, or read.

Materials needed—whether playing solo, at an airport, or with others:

- Folktales and fairytales selected and agreed upon by the individual or group—groups of three usually work well together. If there is a facilitator, selected narratives may be printed prior to the game for those who may not know them.
- Tools for writing or recording lists of significant "things," and responses to them. A sheet of paper, folded lengthwise, for each group—and each story.

How to play:

Decide on whether the group is working on details, or objects, or actions that are plot points—not two or three topics, only one at a time—before the game begins. Participants brainstorm a list of these "things" as quickly as possible—when I'm facilitating this game, I usually give the topic, and a listing time-limit of one to three minutes. Two or more "scribes" in each group record these items as a list in the first column on one side of the paper only. Then participants discuss whether or not these items are essential, and why, and whether the story could be shared without that detail or object or action. Notes on the discussion can be made in the second column, if needed. Participants then determine whether the detail, item, or action is replaceable with some other "thing," make suggestions—which are noted on the back of the paper in the first column, as the second column is always for notes, if they are needed—and discuss the way the story will change because of these suggestions, then recreate the story. Finally, each group shares the recreated story.

Here are some examples of play, using a well-known variant of "Red Riding Hood."

Example: Details

In the story of "Red Riding Hood," we usually meet a little girl wearing a red hooded cape and carrying a basket in which there are goodies for Grandma. The little girl skips on a path through the woods to her Grandma's house. Along the way, she meets a wolf.

The list of details could include:

- The weather must be cool—the little girl is wearing a hooded cape.
- The basket must be light and easy to carry—the little girl is skipping as she carries the basket.
- The journey to Grandma's must be considered a short, safe one, and the family is unaware that there is a wolf in the woods—the little girl travels alone, without any concerns for her own well-being, and she doesn't seem to be considering spending the night at her grandparent's home.

After some discussion, the things that replace these details might include:

- The weather is extremely hot. The little girl doesn't wear a hooded cape. Instead, she wears red flip-flops.
- Since it's a hot day, the basket is filled with items for a trip to the beach: a bathing suit, blanket, sunglasses, SPF 15 sun protectant, and an iPod. The little girl is going to meet Grandma on the beach.
- The journey is still a short one. The wolf is now a shark, just offshore at the beach, and Grandma lives in a beach house.

EXAMPLE: OBJECTS

The list of objects could include:

- A red riding hood (Why is the girl walking? Does this garment have other significance?)
- A basket of goodies—what's in the basket? Could

the basket's contents be carried in a different way?)

After some discussion, the things that replace or enhance the use of these objects might include:

- A red riding hood and a pony on which the girl rides—this would definitely change the meeting with the wolf or,
- The red riding hood is a means of protection for the girl. Grandma can't see well, but she would recognize her granddaughter because of the colorful cape—This would explain the girl's thinking the wolf was her grandmother later in the story—the kid can't see well, an inherited difficulty with vision.
- The basket is filled with: jars of homemade soup, a freshly baked loaf of bread, a bottle of medicine, surrounded by cloth napkins to keep the soup jars and medicine bottle from breaking—This leads to the conclusion that Grandma is sick. Thus, the gruff voice of the wolf dressed in Grandma's gown could be explained or,
- The basket is replaced with a hunting rifle—bad news for the Big Bad Wolf.

These examples show how the plot has to be revised if details or objects in the story are changed. Now, an example of deliberate changes in plot points:

Example: Plot Points

The list of plot points could include:

- Red Riding Hood is looking forward to spending time with her Grandma.

- Red Riding Hood is innocent enough to stop and talk with a stranger.
- The wolf gets into Grandma's house.
- After some discussion, the things that become new plot points might include:
- Red Riding Hood is angry because she wants to play with her friends, not visit her grandmother. (This leads her to stop and play in the woods with a new acquaintance.)
- Red Riding Hood realizes her playmate is a dangerous character, so she runs back home and gets her big brother to come with her to Grandma's house—This leads to a different scenario when the two find a wolf in Grandma's nightgown.
- Grandma isn't at home when the wolf arrives; she's playing bingo with her friends at the church bazaar—This leads to Grandma's return to her home, to find her grandchildren have brought her a new wolf-skin rug.

Interesting ideas for different versions of the story, right?

OTHER SOURCES

In addition to the sources I've given for stories within each of the "A NOTE OR TWO FOR YOU," here are some noteworthy authors and editors whose works may be of interest and value to you. Many of the books and stories are for mature readers. Before you copy this as a booklist for classrooms, or grab a title and begin to read it as a bedtime story, please respect your young folks' level of maturity both as readers and little human beings by reading the stories first for yourself.

TERRI WINDLING AND ELLEN DATLOW.

Terri Windling, award-winning author, editor, artist, and essayist, has collaborated for decades with editor and anthologist extraordinaire Ellen Datlow. Among their many offerings of mythic fiction, magical literature and literary fairy tales, look for:

The anthology series: Year's Best Fantasy and Horror, Windling and Datlow (1986-2003).

The 'Fairy Tale' series, created by Windling with artist Thomas Canty, Ace Books and Tor Books (1986 to present).

The Armless Maiden and Other Tales for Childhood's Survivors, Tor Books, 1995, by Windling.

The Snow White, Blood Red series, edited by Windling and Datlow, which includes some of my favorite collections:

Snow White, Blood Red, Morrow/Avon, 1993.

Black Thorn, White Rose, Morrow/Avon, 1994; Prime Books, 2007.

Ruby Slippers, Golden Tears, Morrow/Avon, 1995; Prime Books 2008.

Black Swan, White Raven, Avon Books, 1997; Prime Books, 2008.

Silver Birch, Blood Moon, Avon Books, 1999.

Black Heart, Ivory Bones, Avon Books, 2000.

The Retold Fairy Tales series, edited by Windling and Datlow—for middle-grade readers, but adult readers will become enthusiasts, too:

A Wolf at the Door and Other Retold Fairy Tales, Simon & Schuster, 2000.

Swan Sister: Fairy Tales Retold, Simon & Schuster, 2002.

Troll's Eye View and Other Villainous Tales, Viking, 2009.

The Mythic Fiction series, edited by Windling and Datlow—for young-adult readers; adult readers will also enjoy these works:

The Green Man: Tales From the Mythic Forest, Viking, 2002.

The Faery Reel: Tales From the Twilight Realm, Viking, 2004.

The Coyote Road: Trickster Tales, Viking, 2007.

The Beastly Bride: Tales of the Animal People, Viking, 2010.

Queen Victoria's Book of Spells, by Windling and Datlow, Tor Books, 2013.

NEIL GAIMAN

Neil Gaiman is known to readers young and old for his children's books, young adult (*The Graveyard Book* is still a bestseller and has been recreated by Gaiman as a two-part graphic novel) and adult novels, poetry, graphic novels including The Sandman series, and writings that have become films such as *Stardust* (produced by Marv Films and Ingenious Film Partners; distributed by Paramount Pictures, 2007) and *Coraline* (produced by Laika and Pandemonium; distributed by Focus Features, 2009). There are many who haven't read his books, but enjoyed the movies that were created from them. Seeing the movies and reading the books are two different experiences (and isn't that the case with most book-to-movie recreations?). Try the award-winning books:

Stardust, William Morrow, 1999.

American Gods, William Morrow, 2001.

Coraline, HarperCollins, 2002.

Anansi Boys, HarperCollins, 2005.

Odd and the Frost Giants, Bloomsbury Publishing, 2008.

The Graveyard Book, HarperCollins, 2008.

Angela Carter

This list would seem incomplete to me without mention of Angela Carter. Carter (1940-1992) was an English novelist and journalist ranked tenth in The Times list of "The 50 greatest British writers since 1945" (2008). Her works were considered feminist and often examples of magical realism; Carter also translated the work of Charles Perrault, and recreated fairytales as dark, erotic, and thought-provoking fare in *The Bloody Chamber and Other Stories* (Penguin Books, 1990). The Virago publications are fairytale anthologies, some of her greatest work as an editor:

The Virago Book of Fairy Tales (1990) aka *The Old Wives' Fairy Tale Book.*

The Second Virago Book of Fairy Tales (1992) aka *Strange Things Still Sometimes Happen: Fairy Tales From Around the World* (1993).

Angela Carter's Book of Fairy Tales (2005) (collects the two Virago Books above).

And if you haven't had enough twisted-tale literature, look for these titles for mature readers too:

Red as Blood, or *Tales from the Sisters Grimmer* by Tanith Lee. Daw Books, 1983.

Twice Upon a Time, edited by Denise Little. Daw, 1999.

Once Upon a Crime, edited by Ed Gorman. Berkley Trade, 1998.

Best-Loved Folktales of the World, edited by Joanna Cole. Anchor, 1982.

Cinder (The Lunar Chronicles #1), by Marissa Meyer. Feiwel & Friends, 2012.

MORE RESOURCES

Please understand that I am not a folklorist in any official or academic sense. I'm just a snoopy storyteller who likes to find as much information as she can on just about anything. I thought it best to let other folks who are like me, not students of folklore but studious storytellers and writers, know some resources and motifs for the old tales, so that seeds and roots for their own versions of the tales might be nurtured through personal research.

Resources are listed in the "A NOTE OR TWO FOR YOU" sections after each story. Motifs are listed at the end of each of these sections, except "Campfire Tales," which grew from my interest in urban legends. The motifs are from the works of Stith Thompson, Antti Aarne, and Hans-Jörg Uther.

Some motifs are from Stith Thompson's *The Folktale* (Holt, Rinehart and Winston, Inc., 1946), and *Index of Folk-Literature: A Classification of Narrative Elements in Folktales, Ballads, Myths, Fables, Medieval Romances, Exemplar, Fabliaux, Jest-Books, and Local Legends* (Bloomington: Indiana University Press, 1995-1998). These motifs are listed in a letter/number format; example: H543, Riddle Contest With the Devil (a motif I didn't use).

The Aarne-Thompson tale type index, which was first developed by Antti Aarne and published as *Verzeichnis der Märchentypen* in 1910, then translated, revised, and enlarged by Stith Thompson (1885-1976) in 1928 and 1961, is a staple of folklore studies. The AT-number system was updated and expanded in 2004 by Hans-Jörg Uther, and included international folktales in its expansion with the publication of his massive work, *The Types of International Folktales: A Classification and Bibliography.* Uther's expansion and redevelopment of the index is known as the Aarne-Thompson-Uther classification (ATU number) system. That is familiar to me. These motifs are listed with AT or ATU before each number; example: ATU510A, the persecuted heroine (or Cinderella).

A search engine for indexed motifs of diverse tales is available at http://storysearch.symbolicstudies.org/.

If you have enjoyed Lyn Ford's telling of—and discussion of—folktales and scary stories, please take some time to visit:

www.storytellerlynford.com
www.parkhurstbrothers.com
www.storynet.org

Her roots are in her culture and stories

"A rich and unique landscape peopled with characters and plots as unusual as they are delightful."
—**Jim May**, Storyteller, Author and Educator, IL

Lyn Ford is one of America's busiest touring storytellers. She headlines events coast-to-coast, including the National Storytelling Festival and the National Storytelling Conference. The power of her performance comes straight out of her family storytelling heritage, which is the content of this, her first book. Here she tells how she learned stories from her father and grandfather—and she includes many of the stories they told her.

"... The minute I read the line, 'One does not give power to those who try to subvert knowledge, simply because it does not fit into their own worldview,' I knew that I was going to love this book. And that was just the preface."
—**Kim Weitkamp**, Humorist and Storyteller, West Virginia

Paperback · ISBN 978-1-935166-66-5
160 Pages @ 6" x 9"
Ebook · eISBN 978-1-935166-67-2
www.parkhurstbrothers.com

BEYOND THE BRIAR PATCH

Affrilachian Folktales, Food and Folklore

Retold by Lyn Ford

Author Q & A and Reading Group Extras Included

Folktales, food & folklore from the African-American tradition in Appalachia

Lyn Ford, an African-American storyteller honored by her peers nationally, retells traditional stories and Folkways from her cultural heritage. Her first book (*Affrilachian Tales*, Parkhurst Brothers Publishers, 2012) received the Anne Izard Storyteller's Choice Award from the Westchester County Library System in New York state. In 2013 Lyn was named to the Circle of Excellence by the National Storytelling Network.

"*Beyond the Briar Patch* is more than a compilation of engaging folktales; it's a cultural treasury . . ."
—The Midwest Book Review

Paperback · ISBN 978-1-62491-025-8
158 Pages @ 6" x 9"
Ebook · eISBN 978-1-62491-026-5
www.parkhurstbrothers.com